SeX, BLoOD AnD ROcK 'n' RoLL

SeX, BLoOD AnD ROcK 'n' RoLL

Kimberly Warner-Cohen

FINKELSTEIN
MEMORIAL LIBRARY
SPRING VALLEY, N.Y.

PUBLISHING

BROOKLYN, NEW YORK

Ig Publishing
178 Clinton Avenue
Brooklyn, NY 11205

www.igpub.com

Library of Congress Cataloging-in-Publication Data

Warner-Cohen, Kimberly.
  Sex, blood, and rock 'n' roll / Kimberly Warner-Cohen.
    p. cm.
  ISBN-13: 978-0-9771972-1-7
  ISBN-10: 0-9771972-1-2
    1. Women serial murderers--New York (State)--New York--
Fiction. 2. Sadomasochism--Fiction.
I. Title.
  PS3623.A8642S49 2006
  813'.6--dc22

                        2006004180

ISBN-10: 0-9771972-1-2
ISBN-13: 978-0-9771972-1-7

For Carey and George,
who had faith
in me when I didn't have
faith in myself

"This is the Millennium of Aftermath"
- Dr. Dre

He's sitting alone on a worn brocade couch in Café Reggio, the place right off Bleecker with the hundred-year-old espresso machine. Shaggy black hair, green eyes haunted by his own shadows, looking like he survives on deli coffee and Ramen noodles. Get my double espresso and pretend to look around though there are enough seats, slowly walk over. Illumination is coming from the fake gaslights, and the air is moist and sweet though it hasn't been raining out. Sit on the other end of the couch and rummage through my bag, pull out a wrinkled copy of *On the Road*. Ignore him and scan the pages, wait for it. When I put down the book to take a sip, he turns.

"That's one of my favorites."

"Really? Mine, too. I broke the binding on my last copy."

We start talking, moving from the Beats to Eastern forms of socialism to the idea of the philosopher king. A nice liberal arts education's done him well. While we're exchanging, I make all the right signs—brush my fingers against his wrist while I'm talking about my favorite artist (Francis Bacon), mimic his movements as he extols the virtues of Mao Tse-tung. He smells really good—a mixture of earnestness and Ivory. After our third cup I say, "Do you want to come back to my house and get stoned?"

We wander arm in arm under the tree-lined streets to my place on Charles, next to the river. Takes off his beaten motorcycle jacket when we get inside, sits on the sofa. "Nice," he says, looking around at the exposed brick, black marble fireplace.

"Thanks. Want something to drink?"

"Sure." Flips through my coffee-table book of Andy Warhol prints, stares for a long time at "Orange Car Crash." Grab two bottles of Grolsch from the fridge, watching him as I uncap them. The curve of his neck is smooth and hairless, eyelashes so long I can see them from where I'm standing. Instead of brushing my nose against the peach fuzz on his cheeks, tell him pretty things, take Rophynol from the small plastic pouch in the bottom of my pocket and crush it into his beer, swishing it around until it dissolves. Briefly wonder what he was going to do tonight, if he has a girlfriend, a dog. Hand him his bottle and sit down, take a joint from the lacquered box on the end table.

"Like it?" I say, staring at the hollow of his collarbone just above the fraying blue T-shirt.

"I go to the Guggenheim all the time to look at his stuff. Even dressed like him one year for the Halloween parade." Light up, letting the heavy smoke fill my mouth and lungs. Our fingertips brush as I pass it to him.

"Thanks," he says hoarsely, laying the book open. Drink our beers and don't say much, our knees, then thighs resting against each other. Looking at the soft skin under his jawbone, taking deep breaths to keep from getting too excited. Roach burns my middle finger and thumb and I crush it in the stainless steel ashtray.

"Whoa," he says. "This stuff is really strong." Leans back, runs his fingers through his hair, breath getting shallow. Eyes glassy, flutter closed then open. "Was there something in that weed?" Pushes the strands away from his face, palm brushing against his forehead. Cool and damp. "Don't be silly." So much easier this way. Tried other things and sometimes they fight.

Kiss right above the pulse on his neck, lips linger for an extra beat. He tries to say something but can't form the words.

"It's OK," I coo. "You're just a little fucked up. Lie back. I'll make you feel better." Lift my leg up so he's trapped on the couch, rest my crotch against his. Pants are damp but I can't tell if it's because I'm sweating or wet. Grind against his soft cock, coercing a hard-on. Fingers on skin, reading the braille of his bones, knowing I can crack them any time I choose. Shirt pushed up reveals taut stomach and wispy line from the middle of his chest to the top of his jeans. Kiss the dip in his breastbone right between his small cherry nipples. Was going to wait, take my time, but I can't stand it. Sit up and give him my coyest smile. Shirt off, I take one of his hands in both of mine, letting his limp fingers, palm, tease my nipples until they're sensitive. Lick my fingertips and run them around his.

"I'm so dizzy," he mutters.

"You're fine."

"What's going on?"

"You're in my apartment."

"I am?"

"Yes."

"Where's that?'

"Don't worry about it."

Nods vaguely. "Will you take care of me?"

Rub his leg under the soft jeans; image of bones shattering drenched in scarlet. Definitely wet now. Grab the polished silver envelope opener from the vase on the coffee table. Didn't his mother ever teach him not to talk to strangers?

Kiss him, my free hand cradling his cheek, work his lips open, merge into each other. Soft and full, tongue too heavy to move, taste of weed and beer lingering in his mouth. I stick the opener into the pliable skin on the side of his belly. Eyes widen beneath mine and pupils quickly dilate; surprised guttural half-grunt. Knees on his wrists now and I reach for the three black scarves, my accomplices, hiding under the couch. Small trail of red escapes the underside of the blade. "My side hurts. Why does my side hurt?"

"Because I just stabbed you," I say before shoving one of the scarves into his mouth. Tie the other around his head, making a gag. Tie his hands with the third. Muffled squealy noise and he tries to sit up but I have my weight on him and he's too drugged to struggle. Beautiful, helpless boy.

My cheeks flush as I wiggle the blade just a little in then out. Blood dribbles, pooling underneath him. Silent tears slide into his ears, tangy odor of fear coming through his pores. Push in again so that he gasps, then slide it out almost to the tip, let it hang. Back of my neck tingles.

He's semi-hard. Rub my nipples against his, nuzzle the small hairs on his earlobe. Can only do this for a moment since the meaty waft of blood coming from his side makes my breath catch. Keeps crying, choking, trying to breathe through his mouth. I kiss him, let my tongue roll around the fragile tissues of his mouth. Stare down at him gagged, shirt shoved up, knife glinting in his side. Grasp the handle warm from his body temperature, and slight wrist movement; smile. Blood runs over my fingertips, staining them.

Thrust in and jerk out quickly. Chest heaves and I trace my fingertips slowly down the straining muscles of his neck, curving ridge of his shoulder socket. Skin stretched over jutting ribs, finger along the edge where his seam has split. Blood's clotting, edges gummy. Sink my fingers and he squeals, jerks.

Get in to the knuckle, warmth closing in, essence invaded. Probing, I can feel the barest edge of an organ right past the tips of my fingers; slick wall of something. Push in, ignoring the sharp wailing punctuated by intakes of air as he tries to breathe through the gag. Want to climb into his skin and fuck him from the inside out.

Try to hook a finger into each side and tear, but flesh isn't easy to rip. Lean down instead so that my nose is next to the gash. Scent rushes into my brain, lifting me and I stick out my tongue—unmistakable taste of thick copper. Every time is like the first. Flick my tongue over the cut I made, teasing the edges, rewetting, making it conform to my will. He's looking down at me, big green eyes pleading through glassy mist. "It gets better," I tell him.

Tries to free his wrists. Worried about some hidden reserve of strength, I jam two fingers in and wiggle until he stops. Pick up the sticky blade again. His eyes tear through the clouded comfort of narcotics. Need to taste his organs, bury my face in the soft folds of his large intestine, lick the ridges of delicate pink tissue.

Lick my lips and slither back on, tracing with the tip of silver where I'm going to cut. Watches me and I want him to. Sink the tip into the tight flesh in between ribs, making the incision. Easier than cutting through the steak at Leshko's. Smile without any emotion, keep working the blade to my own rhythm as he tries to lamely wriggle away. Red wells up, marking my path. Finger over the new incision I've made, dripping blood. Put my hands on either side of his stomach. He's far past sound as I spread his skin apart. The gash...

Ring.

Just as I'm about to come.

"Hello?"

"Hey, it's me," Alundra says. "What's going on?"

Blink and look around. Staring back at me are the yellowing smoke-stained walls and sliding bedroom door of the tiny apartment Devon and I share. Cramps promo poster is curling at its edge by the window, back of the door is covered with flyers for bands we have seen at Don Hill's, Brownie's, CBGBs. Light a

Camel. "Not a lot."

"Did you work today?"

Take a deep drag and watch the blue-gray smoke slip out of my mouth and disappear into the shadows above the windows. "No, the new girl got my shift. Do you remember that last bimbo Mike hired? The one that cleared out the register?"

"Yeah. It was pretty funny when he found out that that wasn't really her address. 'What do you mean there's no 940 East Tenth?'" she says, faking Mike's thick Brooklyn accent well.

"Where are you tonight?" Alundra works as a cigarette girl for this agency that sends her to a hip new place every night. Don't know how she does it—I would've hit the first guy who pinched my ass a long time ago.

"A cigar place on the Upper East Side. All martinis and Brooks Brothers cutouts. We still going out?"

Say yes, and she tells me about her date with some guy named Billy she met at Psycho Mongo's. Only listen enough to make the appropriate "uh-huh"s, most of me ground back into the mundane realities of my life. Wonder if I can get away with not washing my hair tonight if I wear it up, convince Dev to order out instead of cooking. Hang up after Alundra tells me she'll be by after her shift.

Stay in bed a little while longer, missing the bleeding aftermath. Figured out early on that *Penthouse Forum* doesn't write about eviscerating your ideal man. It's always seeped into my visions, ever since I accidentally touched myself while wiping when I was twelve. Bet a lot of people think about things while jerking off that they don't tell anyone. Everybody has a secret.

Devon comes home as I'm attempting to straighten up, kisses me before flopping on the couch. "What a day. You know how I told you we're way behind deadline? We need one more shirt but all we could come up with was 'New York Tourist' with a gun stuck in a stick figure's face. Where'd we put the pot?"

"In the pussy."

Heaves up slowly like he's been forging for the gods all day instead of sitting in a comfortable loft on the border of Chinatown and the Lower East Side where he and five friends from back in the day decided to start a T-shirt company. Watch his ass under black skintight women's stretch jeans bought on Delancey and smile as he walks over to the kitchen counter, opens the tin tucked behind the sugar jar that's shaped like a black cat with a mohawk. Runs his fingers through perfect wavy blond hair, furrows his eyebrows as he gauges how much we have left. Had that same expression on his face the night we met at Nightingale's while he drunkenly tried to remember his own telephone number.

Rolls a nice-sized joint with long, graceful fingers callused from years of playing guitar yet still delicate-looking, like a ball of purple light should be dancing at his fingertips. Leans next to me on the counter with that goofy smile on his face, sparks, inhales. Wait until he's taken a big hit to ask, "Can I get you to come out with me and Alundra tonight?"

Eyes me as he passes the joint. "Where are you going?"

"Mother's. Duh."

"Oh, yeah. How could you possibly go anywhere else on a Thursday?"

Before I can think of something to say back, the buzzer rings. It's a formality, since the locks on the front door are so flimsy you can easily push your way inside.

Alundra knocks a moment later. Let her in; she kisses me on the cheek before dropping a jumble of brightly colored shopping bags by the couch. A puff of (tulle? crinoline?) skirt sticks out of one bag, the top of a black heel out of another. Red Manic Panic pageboy falls into her face and she blows it back. "Hey Cass, Devon. Cass, you should have been there. Some guy offered to take me to the Hamptons over the weekend."

"What'd you do?"

"Crumpled up his number when he winked and walked away. Like I'd really fit in with Muffy and Biff while they drink gin and tonics on the lawn. I think they play *croquet*. Anyway, Dev, you've got to come out and introduce me to that guy you were talking to last week. Tall, messy blond hair. Wearing the army vest and fishnet shirt."

"Tristan? Sure." He grabs the 1940s-inspired felt hat that's part of her uniform. "I can't believe you wear this."

"Like I have a choice. Now put it back. Anyway, more importantly, is he attached?"

"I don't know. You'll have to ask him yourself."

"I will totally owe you. Before I forget, I brought sandwiches. Wanna eat now or later?"

Devon perks up. "You have food?"

In the middle of our ham and Swiss heroes Dev asks if I'm going to speak to Mike about my schedule.

"Yeah. But it won't do any good, though."

"Just quit already," Alundra says, a piece of shredded lettuce hanging from the corner of her mouth.

"And do what?"

"It's New York. There're a million jobs out there. Go back to waitressing. Get a job with me. Let me tell you, the suits would love you."

"That's OK. I'll look in next week's *Voice* and see if there's anything out there."

It's getting late, and like always, we rush to get ready. After looking through all my clothes twice, I settle on the vinyl halter dress and Alundra winds up borrowing the leather one with the buckles all over it after deciding it looks better than the outfit she brought. Dev, being a guy, waits until we're putting on makeup in the bedroom mirror to throw on my fishnet shirt with the Day-Glo Misfits skull on it. Bite my lip every time I see him in it. So hot—the thin material just brushes against his chest, teasing me with the faintest view of his dark nipples. When he asks how he looks, I run my hand down his front, feeling his breastbone over thin patina of muscle, and grin. "I'd take you home."

We hop a cab across town and get out in front of a graffitied truck bay, MEAT spelled in chipped bright red underneath its opening; then head toward the small, dingy brick building on the corner of Washington with no signs that blends in with the rest of the

Meatpacking District (either you know it or you don't). Transvestite hooker with a stringy blond wig leans against a once-white truck across the street. Her turquoise dress with chunks of sequins missing is crumpled, one of the straps hanging lazily (defiantly?) down. She's looking at her feet, maybe at the pump that's lost its heel. Want her to peek up so I can see her face but Alex waves the three of us past the velvet rope after air kisses and we go inside the Versailles Room.

Red velvet ornate couches line the walls, gilt mirror above the mantle and cream-colored paper detailed in gold. Marcella, wearing some sort of black and crimson bustle skirt, is talking to Spider on the couch by the bathroom, which is weird since Spider's sleeping with Marcella's girlfriend and usually avoids Marcella like an Abercrombie and Fitch shirt. He keeps glancing around, fidgeting with the links of his chain metal necklace as she leans in to talk to him. Anthony's got his flavor of the week slid up against the wall; she believes everything he's telling her. After giggling about the scene that will play out when she realizes that his lines are just that, Alundra remarks, "You know if Lila shows up, you should talk to her about a job."

"Why?"

"She works as a mistress."

Glance at Dev, who's pretending to not listen. "Very funny," I say.

"Why not? The money is really good and you're not naked or anything. All you have to do is beat up men."

"...Who are naked," Dev interrupts over the beat of Nine Inch

Nails.

Not as quick to dismiss the notion as he is, but as I'm nodding Balthus comes toward us. Actually, toward Alundra. They had a one-night stand over a year ago, and he hasn't quite gotten over it. Not interested in witnessing the rerun, I tug on Devon's arm. "C'mon. Let's go dance."

Alundra tries to grab my wrist as I stick out my tongue at her and scoot away. The refined decadence of the Versailles Room gives way to the near-debauchery of the main dance floor. The room is black, and the mirrors on the walls make the space seem larger than it actually is. Beautiful people dressed in velvet or latex, corsets and spiked shoes. So packed tonight that a few of the more scantily clad have retreated to the stage with its Twin Peaks-esque red velvet curtains. Stand by the wall, dance to Wolfsheim and the newest New Model Army, sip our drinks. Dev slips his arm around my waist and everything fades to a dull noise as I look up into perfect serene gray eyes, ones that gaze back at me with everything. Want to climb in there, nestle somewhere behind his pupils and just be safe forever.

Funny how we met, seems like ages ago. Dev had, in fact, mixed up his telephone number that first time in Nightingale's; I remembered the order of mine. He never called, and though I thought him good-looking enough to blush over, there's plenty out there.

A month or so later, I went with my new friend Alundra to see the Sea Monkeys at Continental. They were playing early, early enough to use it as an excuse to catch the end of Happy Hour. It was late summer, when the heat doesn't break with daylight; no cool breeze anywhere near St. Mark's and Third that night. Men's undershirt stuck to the sweat on my ribs, as I wiped a droplet off my cheekbone more than a little eyeliner came with it. All I wanted to do was get a beer and go into the tiny bathroom downstairs to fix my makeup.

As I turned to my left to order, I saw Dev three or four feet down the chipped black painted bar talking to two of his then band members. Recognized him immediately (couldn't forget him). Doubting he'd remember who I was, pretended not to see him and hoped the bartender would break away from her conversation with the regular long enough to get my drink.

Crushing out one cigarette, about to light another and then he was standing right next to me. Gave him my "Can I help you?" face.

"Is your name Cassie?" Dev told me later that I looked surprised when he said that, and I was shocked that as drunk as he was the night we met, he could repeat the conversation we had, down to remembering that I loved Troma and while hating to admit it, preferred the Jane's Addiction cover of "Sympathy for the Devil" to the original.

Bought me a beer and apologized. He'd waited for me to call, sure he'd written the numbers correctly. Then his band, Broken Glass, had gone on a tour of the East Coast for a few weeks. By the time he got back, he figured it was too late. That he could recall so much caught my interest.

Later he walked me back to my apartment, triple checking the number I'd written on the back of a flyer for his next show. Called me the day after, asking me if I wanted to hang out, maybe grab some dinner. It wasn't long before we were inseparable, and as soon as my lease was up, I moved in with him at the apartment before this one, on Fourth and B. Our relationship has felt so right since that (second) time. Of course we've had our bumps, but in the end we work things out and still snuggle with each other every night.

About to tell him how much he means to me as one song merges into the next, to see the dimples that come out only when he's really smiling, but Lila walks in and makes a beeline to the bar. Watch her wave hi to Michelle as I picture myself in a latex catsuit with a whip and fuck it, it's gotta pay better than retail. Tell Devon I'll be right back. Go over, tap Lila on the shoulder and she smiles as we both worm our way through the crowd to get to the bar.

"Hey, Cassie."

"How're you doing?"

"My cab got lost getting here. The guy missed the turn on the highway then argues with me that Washington Street doesn't exist. What kind of idiot can't get off at Fourteenth? Kamikaze, please."

Lean in so she can hear me over the pounding of Bi God 20's cover of "Like a Prayer." "Alundra told me that I should talk to you about a job." She nods, sipping her drink through the red mixing straw, so I say, "As a mistress?"

Puts her hand on my arm. "They'd hire you in a second."

"Really? I haven't done it before, though."

"Most haven't at first. I hadn't. Evelyn, the boss, trains the new girls. She's just looking for people who'll show up and look good in fetish clothes. We get a lot of clients. Here, let me give you the number." Takes a napkin off the bar. "Do you have a pen? I can only find eyeliner." Nod no, so she scrawls the number down. "It's called The Studio. Call during the day and ask for Evelyn. Oh, I really have to go dance to this song." Kisses me on the cheek. "I'll talk to you later." She disappears into the throng.

Put the napkin in my bag. Devon's leaning against the pillar by the bar, talking to Spider. Winks when he sees me and breaks away from the conversation. Watch him walk over, wraps his arm around me, kisses the side of my neck.

We're finishing our drinks when Alundra finds us. "Thanks a lot. He wouldn't fucking leave me alone."

"That's what you get for sleeping with him in the back of your car while you were drunk," Dev says.

"But it's been a year. Haven't I done enough penance? Did you talk to Lila? I saw her walk in while the twerp was telling me how beautiful our children will be."

"Yeah." Turn to Dev. "You ready?"

"I was ready before we left the apartment."

"How'd it go with Lila?" Dev asks as we go back to the bedroom. "She gave me the number, said it isn't so hard. They train the new girls."

"Is this something you want to do? I mean, it is the sex industry, hon."

"I dunno. Maybe. It's good money. Would you be upset?"

"I'm not too crazy about my girlfriend beating up some guy while he gets off on it, but you know I have your back. I love you."

"I love you, too."

We get undressed and I curl up into his side. His skin is slightly salty and cool under my lips. Dev passes out right away, but it takes me longer to drift off, mind swirling with alcohol.

Wake up in the middle of the night, sodium lights sneaking in on the sides of the shades, making the shadows play out in weird shapes on the ground. Don't know why I'm wide-awake, except for the fading dream images of Marcus. Sit up, light a cigarette in the dark. "Fuck," I mutter, running a distracted finger through one of Devon's ringlets. Have no right to be thinking about Marcus. Not anymore, anyway.

Crashed into Spike my second day of high school, searching for a hiding place from Jill Barson and her friends, who'd threatened to kick my ass when they saw me smirking at Jill's new (big) haircut during freshman assembly. When Spike saw the Misfits sticker on my binder, he invited me to smoke with everyone behind the football field.

Met Marcus that day. Three years older, he made fun of the cops who would harass us for loitering on Weale Avenue then take him into the alley behind Rathbone's Diner for "a talking to." Wore T-shirts of bands I'd never heard of. Soon started sharing beers on his porch, sometimes until pretty late, while he would discourse on the ways advertising manipulates, or how Nestle got rid of their bad baby formula by sending it over to Africa; their contribution to population control. Only thing I could do most of the time when he spoke to me was nod like an idiot, never dreaming I could ever say anything as profound as he could.

Besides the revelations that fell from his lips, he looked like *that*. To put myself to sleep every night, I'd fantasize that the blanket I was wrapped around was him. Seen him shirtless so many times, but each instance was a new thrill. Long black dreads fell against tanned skin covering wiry muscles from working hours in his mother's backyard, fatigues dipping right below his waist. He'd been dating this punk Botticelli princess named Justine for forever, so he was beyond my reach. Don't know how she tolerated me, unless she always knew I wasn't any threat.

Wasn't hard to see through the shroud of perfection in Priory, Ohio once Marcus pointed the tears out; the small town passed over for the county's capitol. Lace curtains perfectly aligned, electric candles burning in every window. Teddy bear motifs hiding the desperation of never making a difference. Stone houses that had stuck it out through Colonial times, two wars fought on the town's roads. Billings Brewery, haunted by the specters of bleeding Union soldiers looking for a final drink before moving on. Rednecks with mullets having nothing better to do on a Saturday night than drink caged Miller Lites and beat up the kids from the Quaker school or fuck their girlfriends in the backs of cars. Still don't know how I made it out of there alive.

Right before leaving for New York, sitting in my mostly packed room, Holly Hobby wallpaper looking bare without my Choking Victim poster, Marcus called my house from the 7-11 down the road late, asking if I wanted to hang out. Fight with Justine, she'd kicked him out of their attic apartment on Baker and he needed someone to talk to. Pulled on my Converse and tiptoed out, met him in the parking lot. Leaning against the hood of his beat-up Dodge, he'd managed to drink a quarter of Seagram's Seven before I showed up. We walked on empty streets passing the bottle, no sign of life in any of the split-level dollhouses. He talked about Justine, that if she wanted to side with her parents over him, well, whatever; that I was lucky to get out. That maybe I'd give him the courage to escape, too.

Wandered back to the car, drove around until he shut off the ignition in front of the elementary school. "Did you have Mrs. Johnston for third grade?"

Shook my head. "That was the other class. I had Mr. King."

Marcus nodded as if this meant something. Without speaking, he got out of the car and half-tipsy, I followed. Walked to the front lawn of the institution, an expanse of perfect green even in July. Board telling everyone to have a happy summer, that they would see them in the fall. Always seemed a vague threat to me. Hopped the fence, walked around the bright red brick building to where the playground was. Sat on the metal bars of the jungle gym and looked at stars I wouldn't appreciate until after I'd moved, lit a cigarette to have something to do. While we passed the bottle between us getting silently sloppy, Marcus mumbled something. When I turned to ask him what he said, he took another swig and kissed me.

Before my mind could catch up (*Ohmygodohmygodohmygod*), his fingers were running up my rib cage to the curve of my breasts over well-washed Ramones T-shirt, pulling me off the bars, chest pressed against chest.

In a blink, our clothes were off; bodies intertwined, his mouth devouring mine. I was underneath, between the moist dirt and Marcus, the bones in his hips digging into me. While he drunkenly tried to find my clit, I wondered how many couples had been in the exact spot doing the same thing; if I'd played as a kid during recess where some guy had shot his load a few hours before. All thought faded though when he entered me. White light spilled over our bodies. Want to say that we cuddled after both of us moved in union toward monumental orgasms, after he told me he wished we'd done this sooner, that the fates had kept us apart until now.

Instead, we got dressed and he dropped me home. Fell into bed and right to sleep, images of canceling my plans and moving in with Marcus, having curly-haired babies in cloth diapers.

In the morning, drank a couple of my dad's beers before affecting cool enough to hang out in Andy's garage with everyone else. First thing I saw when I walked in was Marcus and Justine, arms around each other on the plaid couch with duct tape all over it, nuzzling each other's necks. Bit my lip and reeled out, pretending that I had to go home for something. Didn't even get three houses down before my chest cracked open, tears rolling down my face in hot waves.

During my good-bye party the next night, all of us fucked up hanging out in Greenwich Park, Marcus put his arm around my shoulder and told me how glad he was that we were such good friends. Smiled and nodded, kissed him on the cheek and told him

I was glad, too.

When I got to the city, I wrote him a long letter, letting five years of feelings vomit out onto the page. Took so many tries to get it all out, and still couldn't come close to what was in my head. The letter sat on my bedroom windowsill for weeks. What if, when it came down to it, I wasn't all that important?

Home from a double shift at my first job in the city, waiting at the Hungarian slop house on Thirty-sixth. Hadn't even kicked off my shoes yet when the phone rang. It was Spike. Before I could ask what was going on at home, he said, "No one else has called you, huh?"

"No. Why?"

"Your mom didn't tell you? She said she'd call you right away."

"What are you talking about?"

Didn't matter, though. There were only a few things that Spike could be so upset about. "Fuck. How do I say this? Marcus died two days ago."

Slid down the wall as he filled it all in for me. They'd all gone over to Akron to get plowed, wound up in a bar near the university. Frat boys started up about Lex bumping into their table and it got taken outside. One of them cracked a Bud bottle over Marcus' head. Blood had seeped into his dreads and he never opened his eyes again. Jock didn't even get arrested since Marcus was obviously up to no good.

Couldn't afford to go home for the funeral. Instead I called in to work sick with pneumonia and stayed drunk for three days.

Look at the embers of my Camel, flat lights from the streetlamps splayed across my hand. Upset with myself for even letting it all run through my head, crush the cigarette and go back to sleep.

Pour one last cup of coffee in the morning, dreading work. Open the purse I wore last night to get my money and a napkin with crumpled numbers scrawled in eyeliner over the red Camel logo falls out. Light a cigarette as I picture another idiot customer asking if the corset is $2.95 or $295, and shove the napkin into my pocket.

The walk from the apartment to the store on St. Mark's is so rote I don't even notice what's around me anymore. Empty anyway, even right before noon, no one venturing into daylight for another hour or so. Only places open are the pizza place and the bodega that sells coke from underneath their bulletproof counters.

Helena is unlocking the gate when I get there. "Mike's not going to be around today. He's going to his cousin's wedding in Jersey or something."

Smile at the idea of not having his tuna salad breath hanging over me until I realize, "Wait. We're supposed to get paid today."

She nods as she unlocks the door. "Uh-huh. If it makes you feel any better, he bribed the new girl to be his date."

Grin turns into bared teeth. It's never going to get any better. Will always be something—a cousin's wedding, rent check, payments to the suppliers. Look at Helena after turning on the credit card machine while she counts the till. Do it now before I lose the guts.

"Listen, I gotta make a call."

"Sure." Hands me the keys. "Use Mike's office."

Make sure to close the door behind me. After two rings the

phone picks up and a clipped voice says, "Good afternoon."

"Is this The Studio?"

"Yes."

"I'm a friend of Lila's...she gave me your number about a possible job."

"Lila...Lila. Oh, do you mean Mistress Sybille? Of course. I can interview you tomorrow at one. Does that work? What did you say your name is?"

Didn't realize it would be so quick. "That'd be great. I'm Cassie."

"OK, Cassie. I'll expect you then." She gives me an address in Chelsea and I write it on the other side of the napkin.

Few customers come in all day, and we lock up after cursing Mike again. On my way home, waiting for the light to change on Seventh and B, pick my head up from lighting a cig and could swear it was Mrs. Manchester wheeling a shopping cart down the block. Mrs. Manchester, the rotting woman from back home who everyone was sent to for a few hours a day so the mothers could do the shopping, have their lunches, let the repairman in for a little extra inspecting. Stereotypical old lady with wiry white hair and cane, leathered skin stretched over bony, veiny hands, bright polyester housedresses.

First time my mother dropped me off, tried to run from the graying skin patting my head and the thin-lipped smile that someone (a parent) would take as kindly, but which I could see through. Musty, sinister house with endless dark corners—terrified I'd get lost and no one would ever find me again. My mother pried me off, and as soon as my little hands weren't locked around her calf, shut the front door quickly behind her.

Only remember bits and pieces of being there, as much as my mind will let me: Timmy Rowan spitting in my Cheerios (I wouldn't eat it, and so I wasn't allowed lunch that day); Kendra, who killed herself when she was seventeen by walking in front of a semi on Route 30; getting locked in the attic for leaving a crayon on the radiator; Mrs. Manchester's demon face amused at my reaction while telling me that my mother wasn't coming back because I'd dug a hole in the garden; being told it wasn't nice to make up stories about good Christian folk when I begged my mother to believe me; Mrs. Manchester's scary grandson staying with me in the tool shed (smell of teenage grease and mold growing behind paint cans) all day playing The Game, my hands raw from trying to scrape through the door; Byron's blood all over the hallway, hard to see on the dingy wallpaper that was peeling on the bottom where the grown-ups wouldn't bother to check. That was when my parents didn't make me go back.

A police officer who looked like Santa Claus without the beard came to the house with a woman wearing glasses and a stiff suit who stared a hole right through me. They kept asking me cautious questions, told them that I didn't remember. Knew that if I ever said, the same thing that happened to Byron would happen to me, that they would hear me somehow and come through my bedroom window and I'd go back into the tool shed or worse, the basement. When the woman asked me again about how he was to play with (as if even then I couldn't figure out what she was getting at), my dad got off the couch. Put a palm on my shoulder and told her that didn't they see I didn't remember anything, I was just a little girl. Only recollection I have of him sticking up for me.

If there was a trial, nobody mentioned it. There was no comforting, no one rubbing my back, telling me the nightmares weren't real. My parents weren't the comforting types. When I'd wake up screaming in the night because They were hiding under my bed, my father would shout at me from their bedroom to go back to sleep. As far as my parents were concerned, it never happened. Another of the town's dirty secrets not to be spoken about. Tried my hardest to forget.

Didn't go down that block again until I was fourteen, when Andy rang my doorbell to see if I wanted to walk up to Weale and make fun of the rednecks that hung out on the other end of the avenue. Andy would later shoot himself in the head after a fight with a girlfriend I'd never met. We hit the corner of Mornington, and I turned to detour like always when Andy touched my elbow. "Don't you know the way?" Said oh, yeah, like I was thinking about something else. Had been so firmly in the back of my head that her zombified hands (surely she was dead by now?) would grab me into the bowels of the house if I passed the dingy white picket fence, was willing to walk the extra three blocks. So was jolted when we passed and it was plain it had been boarded up years before. Looked like any of the other abandoned houses that dotted the town. "You OK?" Andy asked when I guess I was staring too long. "Wait. You weren't one of those kids, were you?"

"No," all of it so long ago I wondered if it had happened at all. "Let's go." Through the apartment door and upstairs. Devon's sunk into the couch, eating fluorescent macaroni from the box. Looks up smiling, and I can forget again. Mouth full, smeared with chemical cheese. "Hey. How was work?"

"Mike 'forgot' to sign the paychecks again."

"Didn't he do that a month ago? What an ass."

Look him right in the eye, "I called the mistressing place."

Puts the plate down. "What?"

"I can't take it anymore. You know how bad it is."

"Cass, you're too smart for that. Rethink this. Please, for me."

"I haven't even gone on the interview yet."

"And what if you get it?"

"And what if I do?" Doesn't have a reply, instead turns back to watching a rerun of "Quantum Leap." Wait until I light a smoke, take off my shoes to change the subject. Which is fine, as he's making far too big a deal anyway.

Next morning, rising to the surface of sleep as I feel Devon sitting next to me on the bed, stroking my arm. Open my eyes and grin sleepily, there's a cup of coffee in his hand for me. Smiles back as he hands it over. "I picked up your paycheck when I went into the store to drop off passes for the show."

"Thank you," taking a deep sip and then another. "I gotta get moving."

"I still want to talk to you about this."

"Let me take a shower first."

"Why am I wasting my breath?" calls as I walk into the bathroom. "I know better than to try and stop you."

"Then stop trying."

Put on pinstripe pants that show off the curve of my thighs, kiss Dev, then walk west, wading though made-up fourteen-year-olds ogling the club clothes in the windows of Bang Bang. They don't bother me as much as they normally would, my mind soaked instead in where I'm headed. Visions of beating the bottoms of men's feet mingle with half-thoughts and unformed questions. How much do they pay? Will they take my picture or do I have to? How many guys come in? Are there any women clients? There's a serious business for this? It's New York, bet they can get someone to kick the shit out of them for free.

Before I realize, the street sign (newly changed from yellow and black to green and white) reads Twenty-Fourth. Turn right and find the address—tan office building with a grid of buzzers and glass doors wedged in between two apartment buildings, a wash of that New York filth that sticks to anything standing still long enough. Wouldn't think anyone other than sweaty guys in short-sleeve button-down shirts pushing papers work here. Press the button.

"Who is it?" a staticky voice asks. Say my name and the hollow buzzer rings. Step into a tiny metal and wood paneled elevator. It opens on the third floor into a sitting room painted black, looking like it came out of some Soho showroom, except for the girls in latex on the framed magazine covers looking haughtily down from the walls. Overstuffed purple couch, black coffee table. About to sit when I hear "Cassie?" The sound startles me and standing in front of a door to my right is a woman with brassy hair in a flawless chignon, fit body outfitted in dark pants and expensive-looking green silk shirt. "Hi, I'm Evelyn. Come in."

The bare sleekness of the first room is an illusion broken by the cramped office. White paint, florescent lights reflecting off the wall. Desk covered with papers thrown in messy piles. Two phones next to an answering machine. A printed schedule and handwritten lists and notes are thumbtacked on top of each other to a large corkboard. Small teddy bear with handcuffs and a bondage collar sits in a corner.

Evelyn motions to the padded chair by the window. "Please, have a seat." Phone rings. "Excuse me." As she's making an appointment, I take a breath. She hangs up and turns to me. "So. You're a friend of Sybille's."

Takes me a minute to remember Lila's working name. "Yes."

"Have you ever been in this business before?"

"No." Purses her lips, so I follow up, "But I've done some, uh, light stuff with my boyfriend. You know, like spanking, tying him down." In the back of my head Dev snorts and says "Like fuck you will" at my even suggesting it.

Evelyn scribbles something on a clipboard. "But you're open to doing this type of work, right?"

Nod and she looks me up and down. "You're pretty and you seem smart enough to train. Do you have an outfit to start off with? Heels, leather or latex dress?"

"I can scrape something together."

"You can expand your wardrobe later. The girls work four shifts a week, six hours each. One thing that you have to remember is that you must be on time. I won't tolerate lateness. Will that be an issue?" Shake my head. "Good. I'm sure this will work out fine. Let's pick out a name for you." Looks at the clipboard. "I could see you as Mistress...Averna. Nice and exotic. How does that sound?"

"Fine by me."

"I do the week's schedule on Tuesdays. If you call sometime in the afternoon, I'll tell you your shifts." Phone rings again, listen as she tells the caller to phone tomorrow for Mistress Victoria. "Also, before I forget, is there anything you won't do?"

"What do you mean?"

"Golden showers, fisting."

"No, I guess not, as long as it's not being done to me."

"Good." Before showing me out, Evelyn double-checks the information I've given her, reminds me to call on Tuesday.

Light a smoke and turn back onto Sixth. Just like that. Thought for some reason there would be more to it. A test, or something. Changed to a job that barely entered my consciousness a week ago. Beating up men and getting paid for it. Little ol' me, a dominatrix! Strikes me as funny, almost absurd; ignore the sideways glances from passersby as I laugh. Tell myself that it's not going to be all fun, that there will be things that suck that I haven't considered yet. Still, hard not to walk on clouds. Excited, like when I was a kid waiting on line for my first time on a roller coaster. New world, new adventure. Anything can happen.

Marring my mood (black slash of paint) is the dread of going home and telling Dev. He needs to calm down, not like it's sex.

Think of detouring, wandering around the Village like I used to when I first moved here and didn't know anyone. Can't walk around forever though, and the more I stay out, the less I'll want to go home. So shoulders sinking, I head east.

Step in the door and Dev's watching a Fulchi film, *The Beyond*, I think.

"How'd it go?" asks without looking up from one of the many eyeball scenes.

"I got it."

"You taking it?"

"I think I should, at least for a little while. I can't be as miserable as I am at the store." Justifying, though there's the tug of not needing to answer to him, to tell him I'll do what the fuck I want to do.

Shakes his head and goes back to watching the movie, veins sticking out the back of his hands as he lays them stiffly across his lap. Light a cigarette and dig through the scraps of paper stuffed in my address book until I find Mike's home number. Call and tell his answering machine I quit after listening to his long James Bond–themed message.

"Feel better?"

"About quitting? Yeah. Not convinced that I can do this, though."

"I may not think that this is your best move, but you can do whatever you put your mind to." He slides behind me. "Have I ever told you that you're really hot when you're nervous?" Lame line, but he's famous for those. Tilt my head back. "Yeah?"

"Yeah." Hand on my breasts, squeezing them through my shirt. Caress the nape of his neck, tracing lines on his back; "Ooh, yeah" as he rubs with his palm. Slide down to the floor, pulling him on top; his weight, heat on me. Shirt over my head and both nipples are immediately erect as the air hits, lips pressing against his teeth. Massages the way he knows I like it, legs on either side of his torso; kissing, trying to consume each other, spit intermingling.

Shimmy out of my pants and take his shirt off, open his Jack Daniels belt buckle, tug down his jeans in one shove. Soft, almost invisible down at the bottom of his back, his high, firm ass that I always tell him looks like a girl's. Press, pulling him to me, skin on soft skin. Hairless thigh parts mine, and rub against his leg, lips opening so I get all over him. He is looking straight into me as he licks his fingers, traces my nipples in wide circles. Sharp intake of breath. Groaning now, one hand clenched in his curls, another on his back.

When I can't take it anymore, going to come just from his teasing, nipples so hard they're throbbing, guide his hand to my pussy. Finger slides inside, *Ohgodohgod*, writhing on the one, then two fingers stretching me, teasing my G-spot like he does the guitar. Grunting, groaning, screeching. Fingers faster, throat gives out this primal scream, every muscle in me tenses up in waves of pleasure. Arch my neck and pelvis, take in as much as I can.

When my breath returns, get on my knees, push him back. Cock is hard, almost red, as I crack my jaw open, slide in the thick familiar ridges, veins on the underside. Stop when it hits the back of my throat, tighten my mouth and suck, running my tongue over the head, lapping at his balls.

Pushes me off and races into the bathroom, grabs the foil square, rips it with his teeth as he hurries back. Blows into the tip to make sure it's rolled the right way before smoothing it over his throbbing cock and putting it between open legs into my wet pussy in one move. Pressed tightly against each other, sucking sound from the sweat in the hollow of our chests pressed against each other, bucking hips, groans merging like our saliva, wanting as much inside me as I can take. Crotch sweat and my juices intermingling, light smack of his balls slapping my ass. Heady wet smell of sex filling the room; dig my nails into his shoulders, pulling him to me as close as possible.

Come as he's thrusting in and out, biting his shoulder, squealing; white goo soaking his entire cock, pubic hair. Right after, he can't hold back anymore and starts slamming, then screws up his face in this way that I've always thought is funny, and grunts, collapsing on top of me. Sweating, ringlets plastered to his temple. Tangle my fingers though his hair, his head on my chest while we both get our breathing back.

"Wow," I finally say.

"Yeah, wow," grins and picks his head up, kisses me. Sits up, lights two cigarettes and hands one over. Bulb shining from the kitchen creates a silhouette of Dev half-hunched staring into space, absently rubbing my calf. Like always I ask him what he's thinking about and like always he shakes his curls and says, "I love you."

Tuesday I get my schedule from Evelyn (starting tomorrow morning, reminds me to be on time). Stay home, doing all the little things to get ready—shaving, tweezing, painting my nails dark red, while Dev experiments with some new chords. Over the weekend, I went to St. Mark's Bookshop and scoured the Sexuality section for anything about S&M. Most were flowery first-person accounts of being a slave, with titles like *Student of O*. Also some instructional books, which I skimmed but it was too hard figuring out how to tie the different types of knots without a rope in hand.

Don't let this on to Dev, but I'm excited as I sort through my club clothes, picking out thigh-highs with a seam up the back, stilettos, leather skirt and top. Have a good feeling about this, getting paid to be a fantasy come true.

Finish packing, doesn't take nearly as long as I thought it would. Poke my head into the front room to see what Dev's up to. Deep in concentration, torso bent over Bessie the Fender, curls hiding his face, only skin I can see of him is his hand and part of an arm. Always been in awe of his ability to go into this other world when he's writing, that he can just concentrate and create a good song from a blank piece of paper. All my poetry comes out as 3 a.m.-just-broke-up-with-my-boyfriend-writing-this-by-candlelight drivel.

Step out of the doorframe; don't want to pierce his bubble. Instead, grab this week's *Voice* from the end of the bed. In the bathroom, run the tub water steaming hot, pour in the lavender bath salts Dev's mom gave me for my birthday last year. When it's almost full, mirror above the sink steamed up in weird streaks from my last halfhearted cleaning, I slip one foot in. Overpowering scent relaxes, hands on either side of the tub, lower myself down, almost unbearable, skin instantly red. Eyes closed, forget about the paper and submerge to my neck.

Going to do well at this. Had last-minute jitters about moving here, and I made it. Didn't go running back to Ohio like everybody, including (especially) my parents thought I would. During our last smoking session, Marcus told me that I was strong enough to get anything accomplished. Would have laughed if it'd come from anyone else. Picture unfurls of Marcus' head in a pool of black blood and brains. Imagine licking the sticky stuff from his wound.

My eyes snap open. Without pause, tightness grips my belly and brain, jaw locks, as I punch the already cracked tile next to the tub. Stare at my knuckles, watching the ring of red around the joint turn white when Dev knocks on the door. "You OK?"

"Yeah. Just knocked my hand." Didn't hit it as hard as it sounded, doesn't seem to be swelling.

"All right," he replies, unconvinced.

Water's lukewarm now. Get out, wrap myself in Dev's old terrycloth bathrobe, bottom half of my hair dripping. Marcus back to back. Fucking weird.

At The Studio twenty minutes early. Enough time to chain-smoke and grab a watery coffee from the deli around the corner. Think for a moment about backing out. Dev would be happy about it, but no—never want to say I wish I had.

Press the buzzer at five to, remember to respond to "Who is it?" correctly. The sitting room is as vacant as the last time, though the door on the far right corner is half-open, with muffled girl-voices talking behind it, breaking the solemnity. Knock on the open office door, and Evelyn's sitting at the desk filling out order forms.

"Morning." She turns toward me and smiles, slight cracks where the wrinkles should be on her pancaked face. "Averna. Good to see you. How're you doing?"

Can't tell if she means it. "Excited."

"I like hearing that. We're always glad to have girls who want to work, since we have such a huge client base. I put all the money into advertising. A lot of places don't do that, you know, but that's the secret to making money in this business. Each girl has her own ad, and I put you in stories in the magazines. Speaking of, we have to take pictures so people can get to know your face. Happens that I already have a shoot set up for Sybille's new ad. Can you come in an hour early tomorrow, around three? Great. Have you flipped through any of the industry mags yet?"

Shake my head no and stifle a laugh. Industry mags.

"Well, when you have a moment. Until your ad comes out, you'll be getting the spillover from the other girls." She gets up, dusts invisible lint off skintight black pants and opens the closet door. Rolls of paper towels on one shelf, dildos (including a big purple one) on the next, four or five leather harnesses with O-rings, boxes of baby wipes, plastic bottles of rubbing alcohol, tubes of K-Y, condoms. Stomach lurches. What did Lila forget to tell me?

"All the equipment—whips, paddles, ropes, are in the rooms. And remember to always take a condom into the session."

"Why?"

"So that when the client jerks off—we call it finishing off—he doesn't make a mess all over the carpet." Nod, embarrassed I didn't figure out that one myself.

"Client gets charged two an hour for a domme session," she continues, "two-fifty for a sub, though we discourage that. I think that we've had two the whole year. Mistresses get fifty percent of the tribute. I know this is a lot to tell you all at once, but you'll pick things up quickly. It's really not as hard as it seems." Lights a Virginia Slim and exhales like Lauren Bacall.

"Paige," she calls. "Could you come in here?"

Paige strides in, wearing a black lace bra and jeans. Taller than me and obviously works out, wavy corn-fed hair tumbling over a muscular, slender body. "Hey."

"This is Averna's first day here. Give her Tiffany's old locker and show her around."

"Of course, Evelyn. Hi, I'm Paige."

"Hi. Averna." Looks like she used to be a cheerleader, or at least one of the popular crowd. Hair is loose but still perfect, no wisps or broken strands. Coquettish blue eyes, pouty lips, slightly aristo distance. Subtle gold jewelry that makes me think she goes to Nell's or wherever her species hangs out.

She turns on a bare, manicured heel and I follow her into the mistresses' locker room. It's smaller than the office, with cracked beige paint in the corners where the wall and ceiling meet. Tall lockers of the same color line the walls, shabby couch on the far side underneath double windows, full-length mirror wedged behind the door.

Two other women in here, taking their time getting dressed.

An older, haughty blonde who looks like she would kick my ass if I crossed her is mumbling to herself as she pulls on black thigh-highs then attaches them onto garters under a flared black latex skirt that matches the bra she's wearing.

"This is Averna," Paige announces. Blonde doesn't look up, struggling to attach the flimsy material. Finally she sighs and mutters "Victoria," through her teeth.

The other, a pretty girl with dark caramel skin and curly black hair, turns toward us. Her eyes and smile are tired. "I'm Cleo," before turning back to the window and lighting a cigarette.

Paige motions to the locker behind the door. "This one is yours. C'mon, I'll show you the session rooms and how to use some of the equipment. You only need to know about whips and a little bit of bondage right now. Wanna come with us, Cleo?"

"Sure," barely audible.

Through the sitting room, notice that Cleo and Paige are in some of the pictures on the wall under titles like *Bondage* and *Inferno*, with captions screaming "Mistress Cleo Takes You Into Her Lair!" Paige opens the door across the room by pulling at the molding halfway down the wall. Long hallway follows, smelling faintly of incense, dim lights high on the wall, our footsteps silent on the purple-red carpeting. Like in the front, there are no doorknobs. Paige pushes the first door open, flips on the light.

Seems so...boring compared with what I'd built in my head. Whips line the same wall as the door-leather thongs and multicolored cat-o'-nine-tails, bamboo canes in size order, leather paddles. Dark lacquered horse with a black leather top fits just underneath.

Floor to ceiling mirrors, and on the far side a throne carved with curled arms, cushions made of black leather. O-rings line the legs, arms and back of the chair. Behind it in the corner is a small set of shelves, can't quite see the equipment (toys?). My eyes run over all of it, and it hits that even though Lila told me that most arrive inexperienced, what if I never catch on and make a complete ass of myself?

Must show, because Paige says, "It looks a lot scarier than it really is. Plus, none of it will be used on you, so have fun with it." Cutout-gorgeous, she'd be perfect for an infomercial. The guys must love her. Who wouldn't want their own talking Barbie doll?

Follow Paige and Cleo into the second room, which contains a large silver "X" with manacles (cuffs?) and a waist-high bed in the same style as the chair. Paige walks over to a small chest of drawers and leans over, pale hair curtaining her face. Take a step and peek in the open drawer—bundles of white, polyester rope of different sizes lie in neat piles, waiting to assist in someone's dirty secret. Paige takes out a few. "They're in the same place in the other rooms, too. Did Evelyn tell you how we meet the clients?"

"Sort of."

"They call in for an appointment. If the guy doesn't know who he wants to see, the mistresses who aren't in session come out to the reception room and introduce themselves. That's why we have to be able to get dressed in five minutes. It's called a meet and greet, though Victoria calls it 'meet the meat.' You smile, say hi and then he chooses. If you're picked, you take him to an open room and find out what kind of session he wants, how long he wants to stay, that kind of stuff. Remember not to take too much time, because the clock doesn't start until you give Evelyn the money.

"Clients love to be tied up," she continues as she walks over to the bed with the bundles of rope. "There are cuffs in the other room and ones on the St. Andrew's Cross," motions to the X on the wall. "I'm not great with different knots. You?" She looks at Cleo, who shakes her head. "I just play around and make it seem complicated," with the soft hint of a Bronx accent.

"Hold your hands in front of you," Paige goes on. Hold my hands out, wrists apart. "No like this, wrists together." Wraps to the forearm, one cord placed close on top of the other, ends tucked inside. "There. Did you see how I did it?" Unties me. "Now do me."

Paige holds out her wrists as I take the smooth rope and slide it in my sweaty palm. Deep breath, followed by a big display of folding. Coils don't line up right—there are gaps in some places and crisscrosses with the tails sticking out. Try to stuff them under, but it looks terrible. Paige is biting her bottom lip. "Well, this is your first time. You just need some practice." Love the way she cheerily tells me I suck. Untie her and she rubs her wrists, says to Cleo, "Will you get on the Cross?"

Cleo leans against the wood as Paige runs a length through the rings on each end. "If they're really into pain, use the ropes so you can tie them tight. The ones into fantasy like the cuffs since they're all fuzzy inside." She quickly binds Cleo to all four edges. "I don't have time to do it all nicely, but you get it. Point is to hold them down and make it look good. Do it slowly. They're paying you for your time." Cleo doesn't look at all bothered being tied up.

"There's also cock-and-ball torture, but Cleo's not, uh, equipped. You should experiment on a dildo in the office. I think the only thing left are the whips." Paige holds the cat-o'-nine-tails she's taken from the hook. "It's all in the wrist," she says, gripping the braided purple and black leather handle, snapping it in the air. "Don't worry. She can handle it."

"I have a high pain tolerance," Cleo chimes in.

"You hit the thighs and ass. Be careful or you'll hit an organ, which can rupture and kill them. That actually happened to this girl at Joie de Vivre, like, two years ago. She got arrested and everything."

"Is she in jail?"

"I think it was ruled an accident. Anyway, the top of the back is fine, and so are the arms." Hands me the whip. "You try."

It has weight, but not too heavy. Try copying Paige's casual flick of the wrist, but it's a lot harder than it looks.

"No, no, you don't go back and forth. It's more of a quick circular thing. Let me show you." She takes it from my hand and does it again, so quickly I can't see what the difference is. "Try again."

Hate being tested. Move my wrist in a deliberately circular motion, but I'm too slow and the tails flop. "Practice in between sessions." She looks around the room. "I don't know what else there is. You know about dildo training, right?"

Nod.

"It's not that bad," she tells me. "Fisting is gross, but we have butcher's gloves that come up to the elbow. Just close your eyes and try not to think about it. Also..."

"Girls," Evelyn suddenly calls out. "There's an open coming in fifteen minutes."

"Be right there," Cleo and Paige say in unison.

Also? Also what? I want to ask, but Paige and Cleo are already hurrying to change.

Back in the mistress room. Victoria is on the floor, fully made up and flipping through *Dominant Mystique*, a pixie-like girl with long blond hair on the cover making a stern face and holding a paddle. Change into the leather halter dress, as it seems like the thing to do, to show Evelyn I want to be here. Slide the black satin thong under, smooth synthetic material sliding up and over my thighs.

Buckling my stilettos when Evelyn pokes her head in. "Girls, whoever the client chooses do you mind suggesting Averna assist you?"

Paige and Cleo nod but Victoria says, "I don't want anyone fucking stealing my session."

"OK. Except for Victoria."

Try not to show the excitement or the dread. Buzzer sounds, that wasn't fifteen minutes. Paige leaves the room. Cleo and Victoria stand and straighten out their stockings. I do the same. Hear the elevator open, muted voices (first Paige's then Cleo and Victoria as they walk out and back in), then Paige saying, "Have you decided who you'd like a session with?"

"Yes, with you." Oiliness slides through the cracks in his intonation.

"Wonderful. We have a new mistress that we're training. Today's her first day. Would you mind if she helps me out?"

"Can't beat two for the price of one. What does she look like?"

"Why don't you see for yourself?" Paige calls out, "Would you like to meet Paul, Averna?"

"Sure," loud enough so I know he can hear. Push away from leaning against the locker and straighten my shoulders, concentrate on not tipping over in the stilettos as I walk, ignoring Victoria's glare.

Don't know what I was expecting (knowing it wouldn't be anything resembling my imagination), but Paul isn't it. He could be someone's father; he could be my father. Less expensive version of a stockbroker, salt-and-pepper hair. Smiles at me leeringly and instinct says to run, call the whole thing off, but I smile back instead.

"I want a session with her only," he demands, pointing a chubby finger at me, pale mark on another finger where he took off his wedding band.

Look at Paige. Can't do this yet. She takes a deep breath and, her voice an octave higher and slower, says, "Averna's new, Paul. She doesn't have the skills yet to do a proper session."

"I don't care. Only her or no one."

Paige looks at me. "Well?"

Fuck, fuck. But who knows when I'll get my own session again? Not like they can blame me for screwing up. "Fine."

"OK. You can use the first room."

Clear my throat. "Come with me."

Eyes distorted behind his thick prescription lenses can't hide the look of wanting to pounce. Bite my lip, turn on my heel as I brace my mind, vibration on the floor of him following.

In the room, don't take my eyes off him as I close the door behind us, trying to remember anything Paige told me.

"So, Paul. What kind of session do you like?" Hoping it sounds forceful enough, letting him know I won't be put upon. Instead, he looks right into my eyes. "I was thinking of a sensual one."

Anger at him and myself for not proving myself immediately. "How long will you be staying?" wanting to stomp down and break the small bones in his foot.

"Oh, let's say an hour." Like I'm one of the girls in the fucking secretarial pool.

"I'll take the money now." Hands over the folded crisp bills he has waiting in his hand. Pause before counting the twenties. Do I do it here or in the hallway? Fuck it, let him know he can't pull one over on me.

When I open the door to the office, Evelyn (mock?) smiles. "Can you handle this?"

"Yeah, I think I can."

"That's the spirit. From what Paige told me, he sounds like your typical asshole. Don't let him get away with anything just because you're new. Don't let him talk you into nudity and no matter what he says, no one does anything else for extra money."

"Are they all that predictable?"

Shrugs. "After you've been in the business as many years as I have you start to see patterns."

Don't want to seem completely clueless but, "Any tips?"

"Let me guess, he asked for a sensual session? The ones who

want new girls usually do. Act cutesy. Make him worship your feet."

I nod, waiting for her to tell me a wisp of information that will make it all easier, some secret that will enable me to crawl into men's psyches and personify their fantasies like a shape-shifter, become the best dominatrix the world's ever seen. Instead, she looks at me like I'm wasting time, so I grab a condom and leave.

Take a deep breath, remembering that I'm Averna, not Cassie, open the door. Paul is kneeling on the floor in white cotton boxers, the kind that comes in a three-pack, and black dress socks. If he can afford these sessions, you'd think that he'd shell out for better underwear. Wrinkled and dimpled, patches of graying hair on his belly and back. Looking at me with pitying contempt, daring me to fuck up. Straighten my back in response. What to say first? Nervous that I can't really do this, reach for a tendril of the S&M-tinged *Penthouse Forums* that Devon and I sometimes read to each other to get in the mood, but nothing concrete forms.

"So, have you been a good boy or a bad boy?" trying not to look at him.

"Oh, I've been very bad," he says back in a way that turns the last traces of my tension into annoyance. Lean in and grab him by the ear, snarling, "Well then, you'd better get punished." Ears turn bright red, like when Devon's turned on. Push that pleasant image out of my head. No crossing over. "Do you want to tell me what you did?" praying that he doesn't.

"I've touched myself, Mistress."

"Mmmm, how often?" walking around him like Mr. Turskin,

the assistant principal in my high school, did whenever I was sent to his office for whatever minor infraction I'd dared perpetrate in his domain.

"A lot, Mistress. Maybe even once a day."

"Once a day? That's nothing. I have a slave who jerks off at least once an hour. Now that's naughty." Walk over to the wall. The whips and riding crop would be embarrassing, especially with the asshole dying for me to fuck up. Slip the smooth fraternity paddle from its hook instead. Turn on my heel plastering my best sly smile and catch him rolling his eyes like I don't know what the fuck I'm doing, that he's just going through the motions before taking control. More determined now, walk back to him, place one hand on the top of his back for balance and hit him with the paddle, though not as hard as I could. Smack is louder than I'd imagined it'd be. Small satisfaction as he grunts. Keep paddling his ass and upper thighs until my arm aches to my fingertips, though his reactions keep pushing me to go a few more times. His face gets red, eyes water, which is magnified through his thick lenses. Want to see marks, broken capillaries.

"Had enough?" As I'm saying this, glance down at my watch. It can't be right—only eleven minutes have passed?

Looks up and says snottily, "You know, the other mistresses usually let me get my spankings without my boxers on."

Knows how to knock my legs out. "I was just getting warmed up. Pull 'em off." Reveals a cellulite-pocked ass and the head of his penis (not a cock by any means). Grins and kneels again. Begin to hit, harder and harder, energy drawing from the rest of my body as the smile disappears from his now pursed face. Hope he'll be stupid enough to shift his thighs and let his balls poke out the back so I can give them a good whack too, but no such luck.

Both out of breath by the time the ache has pierced my adrenaline and we both wait, panting. Paddle shapes on his ass and thighs, almost purple. Good. Fuck him. Picture the grimace when he's back at work, trying to sit in his chair, or with his wife at dinner. Stand over him so that his face is right next to my legs. Could knee him right now and break his nose, the blood gushing out, running down his nasal passages so that he chokes to death. Instead sit on the throne and splay my legs out as provocatively as I can, ignoring the streaks of pain that are racing up my calves. Slide my ass to the edge of the leather, lean back. Don't want him anywhere near me but say, "Come worship my feet."

He crawls over too eagerly after the spanking I gave him. Men never learn, do they? He almost rips off my stilettos—motherfucker just tosses them aside. Sparks of anger surge in the small of my back. Clench my jaw, let my breath out slowly, wait to see what he'll do next.

Swallows two of my toes in his mouth, the third straining as far away as it can. Curl my lips but don't stop him because it's better than standing. One hand wraps around my heel, foot a hostage. Slides his hand on my lower calf, so that I can't move, looks so fuckin' pathetic. Kisses my ankles with lips so dry and thin they don't exist, moving slowly up. I check my watch. Mouth gets to my knee and that's enough. Push his forehead back with the palm of my hand. "What do you think you're doing?"

A glint in his eye. "Oh, please. Just a little." Look at him, wonder if I'm being prudish. Where's the rule book for this shit? Another half hour until the session's up. "Fine," I say, disgusted. "Just keep it below the knee."

Continues to slather all over my shins, prickliness of wet stockings gluing against my skin. Have to drench both in alcohol when I get home. Space out on the liver spot on the top of his head, think about the money I'm going to make off of this asshole.

Ripped from my meditation by his meaty hand grabbing at my crotch. Throat tightens, blood rushes into my ears. Reflex leg out hard and catch him in the chest, knocking him back. He gasps up at me, glasses askew. Want to press on his chest with the heel of my hand until the air flattens in his lung, until he can't plead with his last breath. Instead, step on his stomach, leaning in with enough weight on my heel for him to wince and try to squirm away. Step down harder, make an imprint on his skin. "What do you think you're doing?"

He straightens out his glasses. "The other girls let me do it." Asshole says it so convincingly that I falter before remembering what Evelyn told me. Shake my head. "No they don't."

Has the nerve to chuckle even as I'm pressing my heel down. "Did they tell you that? They have to. All the girls do a little extra for a tip."

He could be right for all I know, but there's not enough money in the world. Grab him by what little hair he has around the sides and back of his head, into his face, "I'm not that kind of girl."

"I asked for a sensual session. Don't you know what that means?"

Narrow my eyes and let the spittle fly into his face. "I don't give a fuck what you think it means. And if you don't like it, you can get out." Screw it if Evelyn doesn't like it, she can fire me; I won't get molested by some guy older than my father.

"OK, OK. I'm sorry."

"You should be." Eighteen minutes left. Wish I actually knew how to use everything lining the walls. Instead of smacking him in the head, cracking his skull, I tell him, "You know what you can do?"

"What?"

"Finish yourself off while I spank you to show how sorry you are. Not that you deserve it, pig."

"May I make a request, Mistress?"

"What now?"

"Will you spank me with your bare hand? I need it to finish off."

End this as soon as I can, don't want to give him an extra second. Toss him the condom and put on the latex gloves I'd brought in. "Put this on while you do what you need to."

Tears open the package with his teeth. "Can I have some lube?" Move toward the drawers before I remember that it's in the office. "You're too demanding. That's your punishment for daring to try and touch me."

He puts on the condom and starts to touch his nub while supporting himself with his other hand. Can't avoid looking as he clutches it, grasping and pulling like it were indestructible, his face turning red, breathing ragged and fast, eyes half-lidded and glazed. "No, you don't get the pleasure of my bare skin," leaving the glove on as I spank him, building up momentum. Blotches spread up from his neck to his jawline; it doesn't take more than a couple of minutes. His poor wife.

Study my fingernails while he gets dressed. Done a minute and a half early, and he doesn't look all that different than when he walked in, hair a little rumpled—could have had a stressful meeting or a few martinis at lunch.

Walks out behind me. We don't chitchat waiting for the elevator. Force a "have a nice day" smile and turn around before the elevator door closes. Face and shoulders relax, head rolls before I head back to office. Evelyn's doing paperwork but looks up when she sees me, worried smile (mask?) on her face. "How did it go?"

"He was just like you said he would be."

"You seem to have handled yourself. Take the bottle of alcohol and paper towels that are in the bottom drawer and wipe down anything you've used. Everything needs to be clean."

"No prob." Back into the now not so imposing room. Black leather under my fingertips as I wipe the paddle that still gives off his vibes. I got through it, even with him throwing at me all he could. Stark reminder that people will try to get away with as much as they think they can.

Took me a few days of living in the city before I ventured into the subway. Was just getting my bearings, remembering the order of the randomly named downtown streets—Rivington before Stanton, Stanton before East Houston (still pronounced it like the city)—and I was convinced that if I ventured too far, I'd get lost in the maze.

It was all so new, so massive; buildings cramped together, leaning against each other like drunken friends stumbling home. And so many people, all existing in the same space without meeting; the idea of neighbors living next to each other for twenty years, going about their lives, never knowing a hundredth of the population breathing the same air, seemed unnatural. I'd recognized, if not known, everyone in Priory, known every inch of pavement there. When the movie theater on Weale installed a new marquee, it was news.

Motivation to take the subway came when I saw an ad for a job as a salesgirl in the West Eighties. Laid my map (knew better even then to open one in public) on the kitchen counter. Tangle of colors superimposed on the city splayed in front of me, didn't know where to look first. Mass of lines insidiously stretched from all points, looping across the boroughs. Took some cursing and cigarettes, reminding myself that I had to do it (there was no safety net) to trace where the orange and blue lines intercepted and split, finger running over stops in Queens before I figured a route that might work (at worst I had a long walk ahead of me); wrote the directions on the palm of my hand.

They'd sweated off by the time I was at the corner and I could only remember a mess of green, red and yellow twisting together like capillaries in my brain. If I got on the wrong train it would snatch me from the safety of Manhattan and spew me into the foreign wilds of Brooklyn.

Chain-smoked to Delancey (averting my eyes from a fight in front of a McDonald's when I saw the flash of a switchblade), pausing as I approached the gaping jaws of the station, graffitied yellow guardrails looking like teeth as they led into the black hole covered with litter, reeking of urine. Eyes narrowed, adjusting as I walked down the steps into the narrow corridor with cracked white tiles and tagged, peeling ads. Straight ahead was a uniformed woman in a bulletproof booth; to my right, turnstiles. Don't know who I thought she was, a guard maybe. Determined, walked through with the fragile air of knowing what I was doing and banged my hips against the metal bar when it didn't move.

Ready to call the whole thing off and live the rest of my life below Fourteenth Street when this old man tapped me on the shoulder. So agitated I almost backhanded him as I turned around.

"Ewe neeth a tookeen."

"Huh?"

He pointed to the woman. "Ewe neeth a tookeen." Stepped out of the way, and watched him put a brass-colored coin in the slot next to the turnstile. Oh.

Toward the booth, the woman wasn't paying attention, instead flipping through the *Post*. "Two tokens, please." She looked up when she realized I didn't know how much, then with the same boredom as looking at the paper, told me, "Two dollars." Slid it through the worn metal and wood slot and hurried through, followed the signs for the uptown "F," hoped no one else saw. Narrow, dirt-blackened tracks on one side, leading into blackness. People were reading, leaning against the pillars or the walls, artfully ignoring each other. Old woman slept on the bench under newspapers and I looked away; still hadn't gotten used to the homeless. Too nervous to see if the train was coming, instead leaned against the tatters of an ad for suntan lotion.

Rumbling far off, then the train rushed in. Doors opened and I gingerly stepped in, all seats full. Grabbed one of the poles and pretended I wasn't staring, amazed that they all trusted this thing not to smash into a wall at whatever miles per hour; wondered if I'd ever be that unaffected. A mom, younger than me, leaned against the opposite doors, stroller in one hand, pigtailed three-year-old in the other; who tugged on her shirt asking how many more stops. Junior accountant catching up on work in the seat beside them. Next, beautiful girl sat primly as she clutched her Louis Vuitton purse, padlock keeping it closed. Her eyes darted around more than mine; where was she going? Fascinated with everything, almost missed my stop and had to push past everyone rushing in.

Followed the signs leading to the 79th Street exit, realizing New York was conquerable. When I found the store (an upscale children's boutique), it didn't ruin my moment that the woman took one look at me and told me the position was filled. Three days later I found the waitress gig, where they couldn't care less what color my hair was as long as I didn't complain about the long shifts or call the Board of Health over the conditions in the kitchen.

Too soon the buzzer sounds. Cleo gets up. "My turn."

After Paige and Victoria meet the client, Cleo pokes her head in. "Averna, he's taking a session with me. He says it's OK if you help out."

Step out of the room, head turning and he looks...incredibly normal. The funny but slightly dorky guy who goes to the Met on the weekends to meet women or maybe lectures at the 92nd Street Y. Stands at the bar smoking Marlboro Lights in...where?... Gramercy Park, Murray Hill. Looks down as he says, "I'm Mark." No catch of too many cigarettes and martinis, no bitter rind edge. Doesn't matter if he's an OK guy, I remind myself. Coldly, "Nice to meet you."

"Follow us," Cleo commands, attitude transformed from displaced angel to El Barrio tough. Down the hallway, into the second room, bathed in the same soft light as the first. "What kind of session were you looking for?"

Starts to stammer, runs his fingers through well-kept short brown hair. "Well, you know, general stuff."

Cleo in a clipped tone: "Dildo training as well?"

He looks at me as a small streak of color falls along his cheeks and he gives her the money. "Yeah."

"I'll be right back," leaving us alone. Relieved that I'll see how a real session's supposed to go, smile stiffly into the mirror on the opposite wall, sweeping my eyes around, hoping to appear aloof. Far wall has the same bizarre curio cabinet as the other room, nipple and alligator clamps draping the glossy wood. One of the shelves holds fingerless weightlifting gloves, spikes sticking out of the palms. (Regret that I was too nervous to look at them before.) Next to them is a small cuff of black leather with triangular rubber weights hanging from a chain off the end and six or seven silver rings in size order, attached by a leather strip. Biggest ring looks about three-quarters the size of my palm; the smallest is two fingers across.

Trying to guess how it works when Cleo walks back into the room with a large black dildo, harness and K-Y in hand.

"What are you still doing with your clothes on?" she sneers, then taps her foot as Mark hurries to take them off. Just as he gets on all fours, Cleo grabs him by the back of his hair, forcing him to half kneel and look up at her. "Aren't you going to apologize for keeping your mistresses waiting? You know, you're very lucky to have two of us today."

"Y-yes. I'm sorry, Mistress."

She pushes his head down with enough force that he has to put out his hands to make sure his chin doesn't scrape against the carpet. Walks around him, laying her hand across his very white ass, rubbing it briefly before swiftly smacking it. He jerks as Cleo smiles wickedly at him through the mirror, spanking so hard that he winces. Keeps going until his ass is raw.

"How's that?"

Catches his breath, bows his head and kisses the top of her open-toed stilettos. "Wonderful. Thank you, Mistress."

"That's better." Cleo bends and runs her fingertips across his cheek, through his hair. "Are you ready for more?"

"Yes, ma'am."

Suddenly grabs his hair. "Good. I was hoping you'd say that. Mistress Averna, could you please get me some rope?" She crouches and grabs him lightly by the throat, pulling him up. "Now we get to have some real fun. Do you know what I'm going to do to you, boy? I'm going to tie you up so that you can't get away. You can scream all you want. Better yet, I don't want to hear your whiny mouth. Averna, could you hand me one of those ball gags on the shelf?"

Four of them, different shapes and sizes. "Any particular one, Mistress Cleo?"

"The green one will do fine. Face the bed," as she takes one of the riding crops off the hook, then puts the gag on him roughly. "That's so no one gets bothered by your little screams. Now, lean forward, arms out." Hits him very quick and hard on the back of his upper thighs with the leather. "Spread those." Takes the four bundles of ropes and squats, motioning for me to come down too. Gives me one of the bundles, unties the second and wraps the ropes around his ankle while I'm still unwinding.

"Do you know why Averna is here?"

"No, ma'am."

"Because I'm training her to deal with *gusanos* like you." She glances down to see if I'm done yet and cold sweat prickles right where my shoulder blades meet as I hurry and shove the coils down. When I'm done, Cleo winks at me and mouths, "You're doing good," followed by, "You like that, slave?" Mark nods like his head's about to come off as Cleo digs her nails into one of his areolas, sharply twisting until his whole body is rigid. Laughs and straddles him, does it again. "I can do whatever I want to you, *cabron*. You can't get away, and now you can't even scream. Ooh, I know what would look good on you. Averna, please get me the clothespins in the bottom drawer."

After I hand the small tray to her she purrs, "Mmm, gonna make those nipples all red and swollen." Snaps one on so hard that even I wince. He shouts from behind the gag and Cleo giggles, then flicks it a few times before doing the other, making them jiggle as Mark grunts and shakes his head back and forth.

Takes the fraternity paddle off the wall. "Mistress Averna, what do you think?" I'm thinking that it's pretty sad that this guy's coming here to get off, paying all this money for what amounts to a jerk-off session. Instead, "I think he looks like a little bitch waiting to get what he deserves."

"I thought so too. Will you help me count out his punishment?"

"Of course." Count to twelve as Cleo smacks his ass and upper thighs with the paddle. "That looks damn good, don't you think, Averna?"

"I've never seen anything more...enticing."

"You think he's done?" Cleo points to her watch.

"Oh, I think so. The little scum's had enough." Coming out easier now.

"Yeah, I don't think this piece of shit can take any more." Cleo leans over and unties one of his wrists. "Because you've been such a good slave, I'm going to let you jerk off while I fuck your slut ass."

Takes a pair of latex gloves from the drawer and squeezes a big blob of K-Y over her fingers. Mark keeps turning around to try and see what she's doing, straining as she spreads his ass cheeks apart with one hand, looking so clinical with her gloves on.

"Open wide and don't you dare touch yourself yet," Cleo growls, sliding a goopy finger inside of him, moving it in and out as his knees buckle. "I bet you do like it, bitch. You'll let anyone stick their fingers up your ass, *buta*." Nods, wiggling even further onto her finger. After a minute, she says, "I know what you really want." Opens the unlubed condom and hands it to him. "Put this on. I don't want your disgusting cum all over the place."

While he's struggling putting the rubber on with one hand, she slips the large dildo (bigger than anything I'd put in me) covered with a condom through the hole in the harness. Steps through, straps herself in and the sight of Cleo with a cock is hot.

While he rolls the rubber down his erection (L-shaped birthmark running down the shaft), she pushes the dildo up against his asshole. "Hope you're ready to be my whore." Positions by holding onto one of his hips while steadying the dildo, then penetrates, stopping every few moments to let his sphincter get used to it; staring at the wall above his head. Forever to get to the base, ass so tight that she has to squeeze a thick ring of K-Y around the entrance after his groan turns into a sharp grunt and he starts to wiggle away even though he has nowhere to go. Checks her watch again and starts to speed up, really giving him the old in-out. Faster, spasming as he comes.

"Untie yourself," she says as she slides out. Using the gloves, she peels the sticky condom off the dildo, steps out of the harness. Then, sighing "Can't you do anything?" squats down and unties one ankle, motions for me to do the same with the other.

After being freed he is quick about getting dressed, turning his back toward us as he puts on his clothes, gives me a twenty before getting on the elevator.

We go back to the mistress room where Paige is kicking off her shoes.

"Hey," she says as we walk in. "I just had the tooth guy. Almost fucked up the Novocain this time. Wouldn't stop talking while I had the syringe in his mouth. Tried to get all technical with me while I'm pretending to pull. Like I know the name of the tooth second from the back." Takes off her black rubber corset with thick boning, dried sweat sparkling on her torso when Evelyn walks in.

"You can get changed if you want, Averna. There's no point in your staying the extra half hour today. See me before you go."

Don't realize how much my feet hurt until I take off the stilettos. Toes curled from keeping my weight on them all day, soles stretched until the tendons are taut. Wiggle to get the blood flowing as I wipe off as much makeup as I can, traces of red lipstick stained on.

What did you think of today?" Evelyn asks after handing me a hundred.

"Nothing I couldn't handle."

"Good, I'll see you tomorrow then."

Step onto the sidewalk and want to lean against the building and smoke a cigarette but then realize a client might see me, so I hurry onto Sixth, with the comfort of merging into the crowd.

A little weird today. OK, a lot weird. But I liked it. And the money is so good—made more in an hour than I would have in two shifts at the store. Getting paid to get my aggressions out. Dev won't be thrilled about this, I know. But I can't live my life for him.

Still thinking as I cross Astor and hear my name yelled out. Whip my head around and across the street by the big cube that I've heard moves if you push it but I've never seen anyone try is Grok, shit-eating grin on his face. Go over to him and he gives me a hug that lifts me off the ground. "Helena's going to kill you for not telling her you were quitting." Helena's been dating Grok on and off since he came into the store one day to bum a dollar off me.

Grok was the first person I met when I arrived in New York, waiting on my stoop (picking at his shredded filthy army pants covered in patches) to score while I was moving in. Helped me carry boxes as he talked my ear off about how his dealer was always running off because he'd undercount how much he'd need and that he really should just buy from the guy on Ave. D.

We got along immediately—maybe because he was also from a small town; grew up in a trailer park a few miles outside Austin. Became like a brother who'd tell me I had a nice ass. Introduced me to most of the gutterpunks, who travel around the country, dictated by the season; like modern-day hoboes, heroin or coke habit in the place of moonshine.

Loud, obnoxious and funny, Grok knows everyone who hangs out, his notoriety proceeding him. Can talk his way out of (or into) anything, big blue eyes with this crazy glint (or twinkle, depending on who you ask) in them, far too intelligent to be on the streets. Thought he was cute at first, but learned real quick that I was much better off being only his friend. He gets by with his Texas drawl and chipped grin. Young suburbanites, trust-funders looking to slum and shock Daddy, flock to him, as well as the ones from around here like Helena who should know better. All wind up supporting him until he gets bored and leaves, and by that time, a huge chunk of their savings has gone to keep up with his coke habit. Been so many of them, no one bothers learning their names. What's amazing is they all swear afterward he's going to come back to them, that he loves them best.

"It was real quick. I'll apologize when I see her. Working at the same place Lila is now."

"Nice. Does this mean that I can get the two of you to beat me for free?"

"Sure."

"Right. Dev would kill me for even asking. You guys coming out tomorrow night? I'm barbacking at Coney now; Bouncing Soles is playing." Remind myself to remember that as we cross over St. Mark's. Leave Grok in front of the piercing shop that loves to gouge kids from Westchester looking for a belly button ring, tell him maybe I'll see him tomorrow night.

It's a weird evolution from the sunny, hippie love vibe of the West Village and Washington Square Park to the dank hopelessness leading east to Tompkins. Air smells different, something I've never been able to put my finger on—body sweat, drugs, desperation. Home.

Don't see the junkie hunched by the mailboxes until my hand's on the first door. Back straightens as I slam the glass open; last one pissed all over the floor. He looks up mid-shoot, surprised, but not as much as I am. Instead of the decaying, sore-ridden face that usually picks his head up, it's a kid, a real kid, maybe thirteen. Stringy long brown hair, too skinny, freckles. (Christ, freckles.) Dirt is smudged under hollow, glazed orbs that stare past me.

"Get the fuck out of here." A request, not the usual forceful demand. He pulls the grimy syringe out of his marked-up arm (not even the dark hairs of puberty yet); a droplet of blood oozes from the hole. Drug hits him while he shoves down the dirty sleeve of his canvas jacket covered in homemade cloth patches of punk bands; big eyes get pinned.

"Just get out of here. Don't make me call the cops."

Does his best interpretation of a jackrabbit. Want to grab his collar and drag him in, feed him soup. Vivid image of him dead on the walkway over the East Houston exit of the FDR Drive, lips turning blue, and I cringe. Grok once told me that all junkies want to kill themselves, but are just too pussy to pull the trigger.

Wander upstairs and start to tear up telling Dev. Wrap my arms around his neck, let him absorb the images. Kiss, lips reassuring me.

"So," he says, opening the fridge after I calm down, taking out two beers. "How was it?"

"OK. I made good money." Taking the slick glass out of his outstretched hand, I give him the PG-13 version, stopping to make faces about Paul. Even without telling him the worst, Dev doesn't say anything when I'm done.

Shake my head. "Don't be like that. It's just that you've spoiled me. I forgot what men can be like."

Sighs and steps behind me, hugs my waist. "I'm just trying to look out for you. I want you to be happy," he murmurs into my ear.

Try to believe he means it, lean into his chest. "I know."

Stare at the pussy the next morning while pouring my first cup. Haven't waked and baked in a long time, not since Spike came to visit with some Humboldt he got from a guy in Dalton. Cut out of work that day and walked all around the city, sun on our shoulders and backs while we ambled deep into the LES, pointed out the community gardens that spotted the gray backdrop of rusty chain fences and boarded buildings, then went to the top of World Trade Center all giggly, Spike taking pictures of the tourists, scaring mothers in garish polyester shorts dragging screeching children with candy stickiness smeared all over their meaty faces.

Open up the ceramic jar and we don't have much left. Grok will hook me up tonight, I'm sure. Pull out the baggie and a pack of Zigzags and pour out the remnant on the bottom, break up the bud that's left.

Know I've smoked enough when I start analyzing the Toys 'R' Us commercial. Move to the shower, running through my head what I can improvise in my closet until I can go shopping. Stay in longer than necessary, staring at the yellow tile above my head; let the suds slide down my back, into the crack of my ass. Fucker yesterday really threw me off. It's all a thin veneer, isn't it? The second that men (no, not just men; people) think they can get away with something, all semblance of humanity disintegrates. He wouldn't have tried that with his boss's fucking daughter.

Perfect warmth as I step onto the sidewalk and inhale the gritty, stale smell of Loisaida. Light a smoke, remember how much I love New York, how much it's not Priory.

Toward the park and the storefront on the corner's been shut down again, bright orange sticker with thick black lettering pasted on the door declaring that it's been closed "Due to the Sale of Narcotics–Cocaine." Way early as I hit Second and turn onto St. Mark's, decide to go to the store and say hi to Helena, but Mike's outside smoking.

Hop across the street before I'm too close and Lucas is near the entranceway to the St. Mark's Hotel. Grok's main partner in crime, he's usually leaning his rail-thin body up against the black metal bars by Trash & Vaudeville, alternatively stretching and crossing his impossibly long, brown corduroy-swathed legs. He'll lean down, so that his face is near mine and I can hear his raspy, drained voice while seeing his skull through parchment skin and smelling his stale sweat, saturated with too many poisons. Only thing left alive of Lucas is his pale blue eyes, and even they are slowly filming over with death. Always think that he can't possibly last another season.

Talk to him for a few. Lizard got caught selling acid, and Acea's pregnant with Ronnie's kid, though she confided in Lucas that it could be Cipher's instead. But he's concerned with more important matters and I head on.

The door to the office is partly open and Evelyn's sitting at her desk next to this striking girl with pink braids down to her waist. Only other chick who's ever come close to being that stunning was this girl I fooled around with when I was fifteen. We'd gone to someone's party in Canton that Marcus had heard was going to be cool. Spike had gotten hold of opium somehow and six of us were smoking the crumbly red powder out of a milky swirled glass bowl with a chip at the mouth, huddled in whoever's backyard, taking tiny tokes and passing it around. Fucked up immediately—everything was slower, like walking through a fish tank.

After we had scraped the wrinkled tin foil, somehow made it back to the living room, all of us giggling, the floor unsteady under our feet. I tripped and landed on the couch that had come out to greet us. Rose-dusted face curtained by perfect honey ringlets held back by a plastic bead necklace and with indecent eyes that had bubbled up from the Ohio River appeared next to me, wearing some hippie peasant shirt that draped her perfect body like Aphrodite at the Parthenon. Her words were garbled, but it didn't matter as she brushed her knee against mine and touched my arm and I knew.

In the baby sister's room, bunnies with carrots stenciled high on the wall. Her on top of me, purple-fingernailed hand on one of my thighs. Lying back, letting her unbutton my worn-out jeans in a tug. Slow, wet kisses on her perfect breasts. Rolling around, almost falling off the twin-size bed. Licking her cunt, thinking it tasted like creamy lavender. Passed out and woke up to Andy (or was it Spike's one-night stand?) shaking me awake, not caring that I was naked.

Looked for her for awhile, but she was like some hallucination. Paul Seiza remembered that she was the friend of some girl John Morle picked up at Lucky's, the bar in town that didn't card. Kept hoping she would appear in a mist one day on Weale, taking me away to the perfect world I imagined she lived in, far away from the obscenities of suburbia.

"This is Brixton. She's our photographer," Evelyn says.

Brixton holds out a small hand and I hope I'm not blushing as I shake it with a sweaty palm. "Hi."

"We'll shoot you first since you're new and it'll take longer," Evelyn continues. "What are you wearing?"

Show them the leather bra and skirt in my bag. "Only have this and what I wore yesterday; I haven't had the chance to shop yet."

"That's all right. Sybille can lend you something. Ask if you can borrow her red and black corset."

Next door Lila's on the couch, rolling thigh-high fishnets up her legs. She looks up when she sees me come in, smiles through caked lipstick. "Hey! I'm doing an ad today, too." She gets up, stocking at her knee, and gives me a kiss on the cheek. "How was your first day?"

Realize I don't know what to call her here. "Fine. Evelyn told me to ask you if I could borrow your red and black corset."

"Definitely. That will look so good on you." Opens the closet closest to the couch on the right, one shoe rack bulging with shoes, another hanging from a hook on the door full of makeup and perfume. Runs her fingertips along metal hangers until she finds what she's looking for. Beautiful piece—wide stripes of thick latex with heavy boning shaped into an hourglass. "It's hard to move around in, so maybe you should do your stockings and the other stuff first."

"Thanks, it's gorgeous." Pull out my thigh-highs attached to the garter belt, slip on my black thong and decide to leave my hair down. Powder under my eyes before dragging the eyeliner pencil across, making it thicker than usual for the photos.

"Will you lace me up?" As Lila/Sybille tightens the stays, I watch in the mirror as it molds to my shape. She asks if I can breathe and I nod. Hate to admit it (no, I don't) but I look good; like a dominatrix. Hair draping my shoulders makes my cheekbones stand out, corset showing just enough to tease. She's polished it to a high shine and the stripes make my breasts seem larger, my legs longer.

In the office, Evelyn and Brixton are sorting photos into different piles.

"You look good," Evelyn says.

Smile thanks as Brixton stands. "Be quiet," Evelyn reminds us. "There are sessions in the other rooms."

I try not to stare at Brixton's perfectly shaped ass, developed thighs in black leggings as we head down the hall to Room Two. Lights are already set up and she fiddles with the camera, brushing her braids away from her face.

"OK. I think we'll start next to the chair." A metal stud dots the center of her bright pink tongue. I've never made out with someone who has a tongue piercing. Quick excerpt of the movie, fast-forwarded to the good parts. Shake the images out and stand by the chair while she tests the lights. "Ready?"

"Yeah." Point to the ring and cuffs on the shelf that I couldn't figure out while waiting for Cleo yesterday. "Do you know what this is for?"

"That's the Gates of Hell. The big ring goes behind the guy's balls, and you sort of squash his penis into the others while he's soft. When he gets hard, he's all constricted." So pretty and I wonder what she was like as a kid. A dork, not quite evolved into the swan she is now? Or the aloof beauty, deigning to sit in class with mere mortals?

"Let's use one of the riding crops." Lift the biggest from the hook and stand in front of the chair, legs open, amused look on my face, gripping the crop with one hand while holding the other end loosely in the other.

"How's this?"

"Perfect." Takes a few pictures. "Now turn around, and hold the crop under your ass. Like that. Stick your butt out a little more. That's it. Hold it, hold it. Great." Raise one foot onto the chair, let the crop hang by my side. "That's nice, too. Might be the one that gets put in the ad."

Takes more shots of me, some leaning over the chair, some sitting on it. A few with the black-and-white cat-o'-nine, some of me just standing with a surly look. Idea of these losers looking at my ad, thinking of me as they get hard, jerking off (under his desk pretending to look at an expense report) and I straighten my shoulders more, smile a touch more wickedly.

"Good," Brixton tells me. "You're a natural at this."

Shifts changed while I was down the hall. After Lila/Sybille goes in for her photos, it's just me and a redhead finishing her makeup.

"Hey," not knowing if she's going to turn into the same gorgon as Victoria.

Looks at me with dusky brown eyes through the mirror. "Aren't you the new girl? I'm Rebecca." Sits next to me after powdering her freckles, sparks a Marlboro Light. Evelyn opens the door.

"Are you ready, Averna? You have a session coming in in ten. William Twelve, always takes an hour. Nick Three's coming soon, Rebecca."

"Do you know the guy?" I ask after Evelyn leaves.

"Who, William Twelve? No I don't think so—oh wait, yeah. He's a cop or something." Picks up a magazine with Victoria on the cover and starts flipping through it.

Know better than to try imagining what he'll be like, open another magazine that's sitting on the arm of the couch. Glossy cover with newsprint inside. No difference between these and the cheesy porn that Kelly Jensen's dad used to hide in the back of his closet. Same grainy pictures, same ridiculous stories that vaguely go along with the photos. Every type of girl imaginable is advertised—how can I possibly stand out from all of them?

Every other page has The Studio listed somewhere; Evelyn wasn't lying about promoting. Start reading a story about Cleo tying up some naked guy in his mid-thirties who never lost his baby fat; she's making him suck the top of her pointy-toed boot. Last photo is her standing with one foot on him, smug look on her face, when the intercom goes off.

"That's gonna be you," Rebecca says.

Heave off the couch, wobble on my heels, hit the button. Elevator door slides open before I can get to it and he looks like he came out of "Stories of the Highway Patrol." Late forties, full head of salt-and-pepper hair brushed back, light green short-sleeve shirt, khakis. Takes off his aviator glasses with the opposite hand, James

Dean style. "You must be Averna."

Force myself to smile. "Hello, William." Lives in a ranch-style home in North Jersey, married twenty-three years. Boy and a girl, he's probably twelve, she's fifteen or sixteen. Billy or Bobby and Susie, some such shit. Barbecues in the summer wearing a "Kiss the Chef" apron, makes a big deal about his secret burger. Always has to top people with his stories about his time in the field ten years ago because he pushes papers now.

"Follow me."

Room Three, flip on the lights.

"How long were you planning to stay?"

"An hour, but I'm sure you knew that." Pulls crisp fifties from his wallet. "I've been here before; I know how much a session is."

Don't hold back the sarcasm. "I'm sure you do."

Back after giving Evelyn the money, and William is sitting in the chair in blue and white boxers and dress socks. "So. What were you looking for today?"

Opens a meaty hand to reveal a small brown glass vial of amyl covered in yellow plastic with bright red lettering reading: "Rush."

"I need you to tie me up and tease me with this." Flash of William's blubbery belly marked with a whip, bright blood oozing from the gashes in the folds.

"Is that all?" Jowls shake as he nods.

"Give it to me." Drops the bottle in my hand and I untie the bundles of rope. "I hear you're a cop," letting the coils fall on the floor.

"DEA, actually. So, you girls talk to each other about me when you're alone?" Turn my head away so I don't let "Oh, yeah, we have a life-size picture of you on the wall" slide out. Instead, tie him to the chair, enjoy watching his fat bubble under the rope.

"It's a very dangerous job, you know. I spent over half my career on the streets." Continue to wind as I get an idea.

"Put your hands behind the chair," barking at him the way he does at his wife to clean off the dinner table. Then I kneel down, force his wrists together as close together as they can go, back of his arm red where it's pressing into the sides of the chair. Run it so that if he pulls too much, the binds will press into his belly.

"You don't have to do that," he says when I start on his ankles.

"I want to make sure that you can't escape and get any of the candy."

"Can I just have a whiff, Mistress?"

"No. Not even a little bit." Eyes scan for something else until they rest on the leather blindfold on the middle shelf. Shove it on him, making the elastic snap against the back of his head.

"Hey, what are you doing? I never told you you could do that."

"You never told me I couldn't. Besides," laying my fingers lightly around his throat, "who's in charge here? You better be a good boy or you won't get anything at all."

"I'll be good, I promise."

Leaning my torso against the chair (careful not to let my breasts touch his back), I trace the brown glass up his chest. "In fact, I may not let you have any at all."

"Please, Mistress."

"No. In fact, I'm going to do it all myself. You don't deserve any." Hate poppers. Did them once with Justine before the prep rally where we both got detention for making "inappropriate gestures toward the homecoming queen and thereby corroding the spirit and morality of Priory High," and that was enough. Stinging chemical smell, fume tendrils burning the soft, moist tissue in my nostrils, explosion beating the back of my skull and brain cells go pop-pop, then total space-out for two minutes.

"Can I just have a tiny whiff? Please, Mistress? I've been so good."

"Oh, fine. Here." Open it and stick it right under his nose, holding my breath. Let the fucker burn his sinus cavities. He throws his head back from the rush, drool on the corner of his lips. Very attractive.

"Can I have more?" Whining voice an octave higher, so I jerk the bottle back and get a whiff myself this time and almost stumble off my heels. Tightness in my chest goes away and after what seems like a long time I say, "You happy now?"

"Oh, yes, yes, Mistress."

"That's good. I hope you remember it because it's the last bit you're gonna get."

"No, Mistress, please. It's not fair."

Try to hide the apathy in my voice as we go back and forth, him begging me for the stupid liquid and me trying to think of new ways to deny. Eventually jerks off while smelling the shit.

Done, I untie him. Back to his asshole, swaggering self, gets dressed and leaves the rest of the amyl "as a present for me." Hold back from lobbing it at his head, think instead of the money I'm taking off this creep. Should take Dev out to dinner, shop at the new kitsch store on First that has the Jesus statuette playing soccer in the display.

Salesgirl smile dissolves from my face as the elevator closes. I sit on the couch, light a cigarette. Everyone else is in session. Looking at the red lipstick staining the butt, chuckle aloud.

"*What do you want to be when you grow up, Sally?*"

"*I want to be a fairy princess.*"

"*And you, Billy?*"

"*I want to be a fireman and President.*"

"*And you, Cassie?*"

"*I want to be a dominatrix.*"

It's a while later (but too soon) when Evelyn pokes her head in again. "We have a regular coming soon. I'm going to give him to you because I'm not sure when the others will be out. Name's Jonathan. Just the basics." Hoping someone else will come out in time but the buzzer rings as Evelyn's closing the door. "There he is. Use Room One."

No time to reapply lipstick, just straighten my skirt as I hear the low hum of the elevator. When the door slides open, I bite the inside of my lip to keep my jaw from dropping. He's Hasidic. Somehow the picture of these middle- and old-aged men with long beards, all in black, coming here never entered my mind. I feel lightheaded, take a deep breath.

"Hello," he says in the stereotypical Yiddish accent. "You must be Averna."

Is there anyone who's not a pervert? "Yes, I am. Why don't you come with me?" He shuffles behind and smiles as I close the door behind us. "So, how long were you planning on staying for?"

"An hour." Pulls out a wad bigger than my heart, counts ten off. Wonder why he has all that money (aren't they supposed to be holier than us?). Before I have a moment to unzip the Cassie skin and become Averna, he is on his knees, naked, beanie still on his head. Old man body, drooping paunch, thick, uneven patches of hair on his belly and chest, back; almost none anywhere else.

Straight-backed, I put the condom on the black leather horse and walk over and place two of my fingers on his shoulder blade. "So, have you been a good boy or bad boy?"

"I've been bad, Mistress," with great seriousness.

"And what have you done that's so bad?"

"I've been touching myself, ma'am."

"And what have you been thinking about while touching yourself?"

"You."

Glad to see he can't see me rolling my eyes. Balance one heel on his shoulder. "That was very naughty."

"Yes, Mistress," he says, voice deepening. "It was."

Grab his beard. "Did I give you permission to speak?"

"No, Mistress."

"That's better." Stand up. "You will only speak when I say you can. Understand?"

Nods.

"I don't believe you got it. I'm going to make sure you remember." Grab the paddle. "On all fours, slave." Raise my arm and bring it down as hard as I can. He jolts forward as the smack reverberates in the silent room. Look on his face causes the muscles in mine to stretch into a grin, wanting to give him just what he deserves. Press my knee on his back, forcing his ass to stick out. Hit him over and over until his startled shouts are whimpers.

Let the paddle drop next to his head (if I'd been less careful, it would have made the dull thud, hitting the base of his skull and dropping him) and press so that he rolls over like a cockroach. "Is that going to teach you to touch yourself?"

Doesn't say anything, just looks up, eyes watery. Then I remember. "You may answer, slave."

"Oh, yes, ma'am."

"That's better." More I think about the double life he's leading, the more pissed I get. Looking down at Dev and I whenever we're on Delancey or averting their eyes from Alundra's and my bare legs on an August afternoon when we go fabric shopping. And here he is now paying for me to punish him.

"I'm not done with you yet. Ass back up."

He hesitates, so I nudge him with my heel. "Now."

Cat-o'-nine next (he's worthless enough for me to practice on). "I said ass up. First I beat you for punishment. Now I'm beating you because I want to." Fight the urge to turn him into a meaty pulp, recognizable only from the cracked remains of his teeth, mouth split neatly in two, eyes gouged out with my thumbs, tongue ripped out of his mouth.

Ache in my calves feels almost good now. Pull the cat-o'-nine taut like Paige showed me; down around, then swing. Tails splay out and down, lands on the bottom of his still-red ass. He'll remember this one.

Focused, I whip up a little higher. Landing (not as hard) on his shoulders, upper back and elbows. Again, and most of the tails land together in a fluid motion right on his spine. As soon they make contact his back arches and his head jolts up. Feels unnatural to stop, even when the welts deepen and it takes him longer to get back onto his hands from his elbows.

After calling him a pussy for not being able to take any more, I sneak a glance at my watch. "I think you've had enough, slave. You know what I want? I want you to show me how much you enjoyed it." Toss the rubber by the door, making him crawl to it. He looks up. "Now, before I change my mind."

Quickly rips the condom foil. Heavy breathing, animal grunts like Dev's niece when she's going potty, then an audible sigh. "Thank you, Mistress." Nod, look at the mirror so I can pretend to inspect myself but really so I don't have to watch as he cleans himself up. Too sad to see him scramble to put on his yellowed boxers, the bib with tassels.

Don't waste any time collecting the day's money; am out the door as soon as Evelyn tells me my shift is over.

Open the door to the apartment and Dev and Aysh are sitting on the couch, Coronas in hand, listening to the tracks they laid down during their last time in the studio. Dev turns off the stereo when I put my bag down and kisses me.

"Hey, sexy."

"Hey, Cass," Aysh says from behind his Misfits-style sheaf of peroxided hair. "Your man was telling me what you're up to. I'd love it if Leaf had that gig. Mmmm, all those guys worshipping her and then having her come home to me? Sign me up."

"Where is Leaf?"

"We got into a fight because I forgot to feed Darwin. She said that if I couldn't remember to feed the cat, how am I going to take care of a kid? I'm like, chill. A cat's not a kid, you know? Kids scream and stuff." Leaf is six months along and I guess is freaking out.

"She at home?"

"Yeah. She's dyeing the baby clothes her aunt sent her black."

Change in the bedroom (skintight black jeans, combat boots and the white tank top that Dev likes because it's almost see-through), bounce through the doorframe, give Dev a wet kiss.

"I'm ready."

Three of us traipse west, through the gutterpunk junkies with carnival eyes spanging, past the condemned brownstone in the shadows near Second, past the guy selling his futuristic dark paintings on the curb in front of BBQs, until we hit Coney.

Coney Island High is a bright red beacon that oasised one day next door to the old Electric Circus club, jutting onto St. Mark's like it had always been there. Open every night, one of those places that'll be good no matter what's going on. Infamous DJ Jayne County's a regular, and there's the weekly Green Door (the punk night rivaled only, from what I'm told, by the halcyon days of Max's

Kansas City), up-and-coming groups and already-knowns coming back for "secret" shows on the tiny street-level stage.

Dev opens the inside door to unveil the typical chaos. Opening band is dismantling, Bouncing Soles roadies trying to edge in and set up at the same time. Girls whose faces can be seen only when the weak multicolor strobe lights flash their way are moving their hips on top of the speakers to the Jim Carroll Band.

Hold Dev's hand so not to get separated on the way to the bar. People are waving money in the air attempting to catch the bartender's eye, while she takes her time passing out cans of beer. Dev somehow slides to the front as I hang back between the bathrooms, smelling the heavy mixture of body odor and stale cigarettes from the sticky mass of glitter and torn T-shirts. Packed, no way I'm going to find Lucas and Grok in this.

Dev shoves back through a few minutes later with three Pabsts in time for the band to come on stage. Pogo street punk, bop my head to "In Your Face" and a cover of "Kids in America." They play a short set, and when it's over, much of the crowd files out. Dev's curls are plastered to the sides of his face. Lips slip from sweat when he kisses the top of my head.

"Do you want to stick around?"

Shake my head, too tired to dance. Dev turns around and shouts into Aysh's ear, who waves before letting the crowd absorb him. Dev then puts his hand on my back and steers me out. Didn't realize how stuffy it was in there until we walk into the corridor and I gulp a breath full of cool air.

Streets are close to empty after we turn off St. Mark's, everyone already at their destination. Even the corner dealer is somewhere else tonight. Wrap my arm around Dev's and lean on his shoulder.

"I love you."

"I love you."

Before I can put my keys on the counter, he starts chewing on my neck from behind. Quickly plummet from hazy happiness to wanting to punch him in the neck. Push his arms off me with my elbows.

"Can you just wait a minute?"

Takes a step back. "Sorry."

"I didn't mean it like that. I've...just had a long day." Empty my pockets, get out a glass and pour a quarter full of vodka before remembering that we have no juice. Crankier, substitute Pepsi, but it's just not the same. Force myself to calm down, and kiss Dev on the cheek by the sink. "I'm just really tired."

Home after shopping with Alundra for work clothes (lots of leather, splurge on a latex skirt like the one Victoria has, Lucite stilettos). Dev turns with a huge grin. "Cheesy pasta night." His specialty is cooked noodles mixed with whatever end of cheeses we have in the house, melted together, pasta and cheese a gluey, gooey glob.

"Whaddya think?" After we've sat down and I take the first mouthful.

"Not bad. Swiss?"

"Picked some up on the way home. You haven't been in the mood the last few days, but I was going to ask how the job was going."

Is he going to ask me every day? Stare at him straight in the eyes. "It's great." We don't talk for the rest of dinner.

Afterward Dev asks if I want to watch *The Toxic Avenger* again. He's sitting up on the couch and I lie sideways, leaning my head into his chest as I prop myself up with my elbow. Not even at the part yet where Melvin gets dumped in toxic waste when I get a whiff of Dev's scent and (contrition more than desire) hook my finger into his T-shirt and pull down, exposing some of the delicate skin stretched over his breastbone, slide my tongue out from between my lips. Palm across his nipples until hard, slight tug on my hair as hand urges my lips into his chest. Pull his shirt off, mine on the floor next to his. Kiss under his earlobe, wetting the soft fuzz there. Warmth, smell, way his muscles slightly tense, all of it so familiar, my body reverting to the sensations.

Hand reaches behind and unhooks my bra in a smooth movement. Skin melding to skin and I forget about the why. Force through from my mind, press my pelvis into his, work my way to his lips, sweet tinge of his saliva.

Flips me so I'm lying on the couch. "My turn," he grins. Tracing and then sucking around my nipples until they're hard. Groan, tongue licking his lips, pelvis bucking into his rib cage, rubbing against as he squeezes, pulls at the other nipple. Stickiness on my outer lips. Wiggles me out of my jeans, leaving electric trails as my fingers run along his ribs, hips, outer thigh. Fingers on my cunt.

"Ooh, somebody's wet."

"I need you. Now."

Pauses since the usual routine involves me getting eaten out first. "Let me get a condom."

"Fuck it. Now." Push his unbuttoned jeans to the middle of his thighs. Hot, hard, soft-skinned cock pressing against. Dig my nails into his shoulders as he enters me, so wet now that it spills over as soon as he presses the head against my hole, running down the crack toward my ass. Shaft stretching the muscles in my vagina, filling it, dull ache of him thrusting against my ovaries, driving in until his pubic hair rubs my lips. Takes his time, but not before I've had a wailing orgasm.

Not in the cuddling mood afterward. Pull away from his arm slung casually over my waist once we're in bed. Can feel him tensed a few inches from me but it's too easy to ignore as I drift off.

Regret deciding to walk to work when Sixth becomes almost impossible to weave through, filled with window-shoppers and sidewalk café brunchers, *New York Times* on one side of the place settings, bottles of San Pellegrino on the other.

Evelyn gives me an alligator smile when I walk in. "Congratulations on getting so many clients lately. Do you feel like you're getting the hang of this?"

"A little."

"You're being too modest. I have a feeling you'll do well here. Your photos are coming out Monday in *Adam & Eve* and in *The Vault* in a few weeks. I bet you won't be sitting down for more than an hour."

"Looking forward to it." Can't think of anything else to say as I glance at the corners of the bulletin board. "I'm going to get ready in case we have a walk-in."

Evelyn must have jinxed me by talking about the ads because it's my slowest day. Throat hurts as I light yet another cigarette by the time early afternoon hits, kick myself for not bringing a book; flipped through all the "industry mags" hours ago.

Cleo plops down next to me after one of her sessions. "So how's it going?"

Trying (doing a poor job) not to be hard on myself for having no sessions (haven't been here long, my ads aren't even out yet), "It's going good. Slow today."

"Yeah, we all have them. Can I get a smoke off of you?"

"How long have you been doing this?" handing her a cigarette.

"I guess about a year and a half now." Pauses. "Wow, can't believe it's been that long." She looks down at her nails, and I wonder if she's told everybody in her life, or no one, what she does. Want to ask her what she wanted to be, if this is a stepping-stone to something. Instead, "How's your dating life, if you don't mind me asking? I mean, has the job fucked it up?"

"There's a point where you either let it affect you or you don't. The ones that do," taking a hard drag, "don't stay very long." Unbuckles her heels and kicks them off, crushing the cigarette out as she leans back. "Why? Is the job getting to you?"

Shake my head. "Just asking."

Evelyn opens the door. "There's a regular coming in a few. Ben, easy hour."

Ben's in his early 30s, short brown hair, gold-rimmed glasses, corduroy jacket with leather patches on the elbows. Harmless, smiles after he picks me for his session.

Lead him down the hall and close the door; he presses his glasses up the bridge of his nose with the furtive concentration of an IRS agent in the midst of an audit. "Ma'am, if it's alright, I like to be told why the Irish are better than Italians. Everything you can throw at me. The more degrading, the better. I'd also...desire a little dildo training with the verbal abuse. Does that please you, Mistress?"

Does it matter? "Of course. Let me collect your tribute and get the equipment from the office.

"So," I say as he counts out the bills, "you must be Italian."

Looks at me like I'm out of my mind. "No, Greek."

In the office, drop the bills next to Evelyn's hand. "What do I need for dildo training?"

"Two condoms. Take the smaller harness over there, and I think that dildo will work. And don't forget a tube of K-Y."

Back in the room, Ben's already naked, kneeling next to the throne. Put the equipment by the chair and sit, crossing my legs in front of his kneeling body so my stockings make that distinct shushing sound. "So, why Irish are better than Italians." His eyes are rapt, and I quickly realize that I am so the wrong person to do this. None of my friends ever spoke that way, my parents only in the haziest terms (my dad calling Willis Adams a nigger whenever the Browns lost). But then, Priory is 99 percent white, so it wasn't because of any great feats of political correctness.

"Irish men are nice and clean and...Wops are hairy and greasy. Plus they all smell like pizza. And work for the Mafia." Not a minute in and I've thought of every stereotype I can muster.

"Yes, that's very true, Mistress."

"And they're stupid. I don't think anything good has come out of Italy in the past hundred years."

"But ma'am, if I may be bold enough to ask, what good has come out of Ireland in the past hundred years?"

"U2?"

Entire session is excruciating. Tripping over my words, repeating that Italians are stupid at least fifteen times. At least he won't ask for me again.

Finally, finally, stand up with ten minutes left. "I think it's time for me to make my point." Look at the harness, lined with studs and held together with metal O-rings like it fell out of some heavy metal porn. Let me not fuck up this part at least.

I've never had anal—even the idea of anything going up my ass freaks me out. Dev fumblingly attempted it one steamy July night after we had taken two moons of ecstasy that Grok had passed to me at Brownies, but even with the serotonin rushing out of our brains and through our bodies, he only got the tip of his head in before I squealed and pushed away.

Slide the thick rubber cock (with lifelike veins!) through, wiggle it up and down (to check what? But seems like the thing to do), belt it tightly around my waist. Don't need to look down to feel the surge of power. I have a cock. Freud was right.

Toss Ben one of the condoms. "Put this on." With no hesitation, he forces the condom over his withered penis, then gets down on all fours. Open the red foil and roll the unlubricated latex down my synthetic cock. K-Y in hand, I step behind him. Glance at myself in the mirror, and goddamn it looks good and I want to see it, to see the grimaces and soft sighs of release as I dive and force.

Kneel behind my guinea pig and slather on the clear gel. Kick his knees out with mine and spread his cheeks apart until I can see the small black space in the middle of his asshole. Grab the base of my cock (word mulls over my brain like the mead Alundra brought us back from the Renn Faire one year) and line it up carefully. Press the tip gently, slight resistance, pleasurable pressure as the first bit disappears inside.

Hold his hips, plunge in hard as he jerks forward. I feel like a god. Want to burst his insides open, pierce his esophagus. Pull out so just the head is in, sphincter grabbing. Like I knew, like I always knew, I fuck.

"You like that, don't you, you little bitch, huh? You Irish-loving piece of shit." Hands move up and down his not bad–sized penis, savoring it. No noise except for the wet sound of the K-Y around his sphincter and the soft thump of me banging against his hips. Smell of sex overpowers my nostrils, head bobbing up and down. Soon his whole body convulses. Pissed at him for coming too soon, pull out as hard as I can, satisfied to hear him wince.

Glad I remembered to put on gloves; it's a total mess. Ass has K-Y smeared all over the place, traces of shit at the end of the dildo. Goo even up over the few millimeters of rubber dick not covered by the condom, smeared onto the harness. Gingerly, so I don't get any on my outfit, I unbuckle the harness and step out. Wipe what's most obvious with baby wipes; will clean the rest down with alcohol after he leaves. Walk him to the door silently, anxious for this day to be over.

Devon isn't home yet and I could use a nap to erase the day. Scrawl a note to him on the back of a flyer for his next gig (Saturday at CB's opening for L.E.S. Stitches) asking to wake me when he gets in. Don't bother to take anything off except my shoes before climbing into bed, pass out as soon as I shut my eyes.

And I'm sitting on the floor of my bedroom back home, but in the way that's only understandable in dreams; no doors, bare except for a small table off to the side. A woman I've never seen before steps through the wall. Blacker than void hair to her waist, perfect pale mask of skin, mouth lusher than a poppy field, curves like Jayne Mansfield. She's barefoot, wearing skintight pants and a blood-colored bustier that makes her soft breasts swell up in arks, pale blue veins crisscrossing.

Can see the bones in her feet, delicate as a cat's, as she lifts them, stopping a pace from where I'm sitting cross-legged. One hip forward, head tilted so that her hair drapes her shoulders and waist, a smile for an invitation. With long fingernails, she unhooks her top. Her breasts could've been the inspiration for a Roman statue, large and firm, her dark nipples pointing straight forward.

Unbuttons her pants, flesh smooth except for a trimmed line of black hair. Spreads her legs apart, beckoning. Crawl until I'm face-to-face with her cunt. Rub just the tip my nose against her sticky-wet slit, the musky sex smell washing over me like a fog. Part her lips, and just like I knew it would be, underneath is bright pink, slick and shiny. Lap at her hole, tilting my head so I'm stimulating all of her at once, tonguing the moist walls of her vagina, drinking the wetness.

Hands on my shoulders, pulling me to her as she bucks her hips, moaning. Throbbing now, burying my face so deep I can't breathe. Surrounded by wet and soft and her moans don't stop, but get louder and deeper until they reverberate. Can't see, but I know that out of my fingertips have grown talons.

Hands along the outside of her thighs, squeezing as I go up. "Yes, oh yes darling" she breathes. Still at her blood-engorged clit, licking around when I slide one fingerblade inside her juicy rich folds up to the knuckle, nails pushing through firmly. Head just underneath, catching blood mixed with dribbling juices. Wrap my other arm around her so she can't move. Still hooked (straight through to her kidneys or maybe small intestine), I tug down, slitting everything until something rips free. Pull my nail out of her bloody cunt along with glistening, messy ovaries looking like they do in freshman bio textbook drawings. Put the whole bloody thing in my mouth. Bitter and soft, it squishes through my teeth like octopus.

Pulled out of it by Dev, shaking my shoulder hard. "Cassie, Cassie."

Groggy, pissed. "What?"

"You were making all these weird noises. I thought you were

having a nightmare."

"No, no," rubbing my eyes. "I'm OK. What time is it?"

"Eleven," he says, sitting on the edge of the bed, stroking my hair and looking down at me.

"Why didn't you wake me?"

"Because you were looking so peaceful. Well, until you started this."

Sit up. "Now I have no time to get ready."

"Let me make you some coffee."

Angry, I slide from his touch and swing out of bed. "I'll get it."

After much convincing on Dev's part and gritted teeth on mine, we wind up at Marz Bar, drinking warm Rolling Rocks. Know many of the regulars, which is strange since we hardly ever go here. When the bar gets too packed to breathe with its usual mix of elderly men far past being able to be classified as drunks and old-school punks trying to escape the gentrification that's been encroaching, we split.

Slow tipsy walk home, followed by uninvolved sex, listening to the Clash playing in the apartment next door before forcing a small orgasm, waiting for Dev to do the same. Alcohol's deadened my senses and just not into it tonight, want to be left alone.

As soon as my ads come out, clients start calling for me, and most days I can't leave without working a minimum of three to four sessions. Dev doesn't complain about the money and I stop mentioning anything deeper than what I've ordered for lunch. In fact, we don't talk much at all. Wish I could tell him about how often I walk out of there with anger and disgust (tell myself every day that it isn't an example of the whole male world, each time needing to convince myself more). But he'll just tell me to quit, and that's not what I need. I need him to understand why.

One night, hurrying down the Bowery to CB's to see the Spider Cunts (BitchCat and Sewage opening), Dev lagging fifteen or twenty feet behind. Annoyed with him for taking me to 7B—never liked the place—and for taking too long leaving the bar (was it crucial he speak to every single person on our way out?). Never mind that he knows I've been waiting a long time to see this show.

"Cass, you want to slow down?"

Don't answer, keep moving.

"Cassie."

"What?"

"I said slow down."

Stand and wait the few seconds for him to catch up. "There, happy? Can we go now?"

"You don't have to get so nuts, it's only a couple of blocks. We'll make it."

"Do you know what time the doors opened? Eight. And what time is it now? Wait, don't strain yourself—it's almost nine. Which means that by the time we pay and get in, I'll definitely miss Sewage. You know I've been wanting to see them play 'Adolf Giuliani.' Why don't you just go home and let me enjoy what I can of the night?" I continue south, Dev a few steps behind me. I stop. "I wasn't kidding. Go home, go to another bar, whatever."

"No, Cass. I'm out with you tonight."

"Don't do me any favors." Please, please leave me be, give me some space.

"Cut it out. You're wasting more time."

"I'm not moving until you leave."

"You're being ridiculous."

"Then go. I'll see you at home later." Start walking away, but he's still following.

"Go away."

"No."

Get right in his face. "Get the fuck away from me. Leave me alone."

"Cassie." Puts his hand on my forearms to calm me down, but the contact sends me over the edge. In less than a blink, my hands are on his chest pushing as hard as I can. "Get away from me." He holds his footing, but I have adrenaline on my side, and the second push sends him into the street. He charges back and grabs my wrists, but I shove him back into the street, six inches from a passing cab. Step back and look at each other.

"I'm sorry," I say, but I'm not.

Having my morning coffee on a Thursday before work when I realize that I'm way late on my period. When I first started getting it at thirteen, I'd keep track by drawing large red X's on my wall calendar. My father saw the X's and accused me of counting down to some mastermind plan to run away or have my friends loot their house and kill them, so I stopped.

Pull on semi-dirty clothes and hike up to the ancient pharmacy on A while trying to count back days. Store sign hasn't changed since the early sixties; medicine and perfume bottles, sun-bleached boxes of Ace bandages and a wheelchair crowd the front window.

Two shelves of pregnancy tests under the chipped Formica counter, cheerily unappetizing under the fluorescent glare in their purple and pink boxes, the pharmacist in a cheap white smock peering over the counter to make sure I'm not shoplifting.

Pick the most generic and head back up to the apartment, where I pee on the stick. Immediately there are two bright pink lines where there was one. Check the instructions again even though it's not rocket science and lean my head against the wall, close my eyes. Fuck. That one time, so stupid of us. I've always wanted kids, but as an abstract idea, like owning a home. I can't keep this, can I?

Scorpions pinch the inside of my skull as I push the memorized numbers into the phone. Dev picks up on the second ring. "Wynborne Graphics, Devon Symes speaking."

"It's me."

"Hey. What's going on?" Surprised, as I never call the office.

"I'm pregnant."

"Ha-ha."

"I'm not kidding."

"Stay right there. I'm coming home."

"But I have to go to work."

"Fuck work. Tell them you're sick."

"I can't."

"Yes, you fucking can."

"OK, OK. I'll be here." Hang up. Need a smoke. But I can't, I'm pregnant. Dial work and Evelyn's tone gets icy when I tell her I'm too sick to come in, tries to convince me until she realizes I'm not budging; says she hopes I feel better before quickly hanging up.

A little parasite inside me, feel like I'm in *Aliens*. Pacing and staring out the window, I catch myself absently rubbing my stomach. Could this be all right? People have done this younger with a lot less. It could be beautiful and smart. There'd be a bond, a special bond that I didn't have with my parents. I'd be a mother. A child to play with, to guide, to watch grow up. And Dev...Dev would make the perfect father.

Thinking about where we'd put the cradle when Dev bursts through the door.

"Can I see it?"

"The test? I think I threw it in the garbage. It's got my pee on it."

"I don't care. I've cleaned up your vomit," he says as he walks into the bathroom, followed by a shout as he rushes back out, picks me up and swings me around. "We're going to have a baby!"

"So, you're happy about this."

"Hell, yeah. I mean, if that's what you want."

"I think...I think so."

"Are you sure?"

Envision holding a little bundle, of Dev teaching a son with the same cheekbones as him chords on a kid-sized guitar. "I'm sure."

"I know we weren't planning this, but maybe that's OK. My job's steady and..." Puts me down as his eyes darken. "Cassie, you're going to have to quit work."

Why is that the first thing? "No, I don't. Not yet. We've got to save up a lot."

"Yeah, but..."

"I have to work to pay for the doctor bills, you know. I haven't had insurance since Priory."

"Maybe I can figure something out with Marlon about putting you on my plan. I want you to find a doctor tomorrow. When was the last time you saw one?" His nagging would normally drive me out of the room, but realize he's just trying to look out for me.

Light turns on like it used to as he puts his palm on my stomach, looks into my eyes. That's what convinces me that this is a Good Thing. Know, despite everything, that Dev is who I should be with, that he loves as close to unconditionally as anyone ever will. "You're going to have my child. Those little cells inside are a combination of us."

"We've decided, huh?" Smile.

Pause. "Yeah, if that's what you want." Kisses me when I nod. "We have so much to do before then. When are we going to tell people? My family's going to be so excited."

"I don't want to tell anyone yet. Too soon."

Hugs me close. "That's fine by me. Whatever you want."

Days meld and it doesn't seem long before my belly starts to curve. I can feel her. Not kicking yet, but she's there, a part of me. Dream about her, looking just like me. I'll brush her hair, take her to the jungle gym in Tompkins Square Park, teach her how to read. Even start talking to her, telling Karen how much her parents love her, how happy she's going to be.

According to the books Dev brings home (*What to Expect When You're Expecting*, *Complete Book of Pregnancy and Childbirth*, *Spiritual Midwifery*, which gets thrown in the corner) and the OB-GYN on Allen, the whole pregnancy is going well except for a little anemia, which has Dev making me eat liver and onions once a week at Kiev. Quitting smoking isn't easy, but Dev goes onto the landing, and I somehow manage (after the first fits, with Dev leading me away from the garbage can looking for butts).

We make lists of baby names, reading them aloud to each other, crossing off the ones that invoke a shaking head or a disgusted face. I throw out Gwar and Doyle to see the look on Dev's face, but he won't budge on a normal name. "What if she grows up and wants to be a stockbroker?" Tell him that it's genetically impossible for any child of mine to be a stockbroker, but if she did she'd be the stockbroker with the coolest name. Eventually we settle on Karen (for Karen Black) or Sid.

Hormones overtake my body. Leaf, who had a gorgeous baby girl, Myrrh, with the biggest sapphire eyes, often gets calls from me. She reassures that I'm not going crazy, that it's OK to laugh and then instantly cry, or crave the weirdest foods (like turnips, which I'd never had before, but one night couldn't do without). I'm bloated, too tired to go out, and I can't drink or smoke, which makes me stir-crazy. There are only so many movies from Kim's

Video a person can watch.

Getting dressed one night on our way to grab dinner at Yaffa's, Dev notices that I'm having trouble buttoning my jeans. "This will be my last week," I tell him. I promised him I'd quit when I really started to show. Can't be good for the baby, and who wants a session with a pregnant mistress? (Well, actually...)

Though the baby's bringing me and Dev closer, things are falling apart in other ways. Sex is even more nonexistent than before, and talking about anything besides my latest doctor's visit or Bradley versus Lamaze ends in either a fight or cold silence. I've given up trying to tell him anything, easier not to talk. If it weren't for the pregnancy, I know we'd be separated.

Start pushing him to go out with his friends so his face isn't hovering over me, asking me how I am. It's that or slap it away and I don't want to do that. Like a skipping record I repeat to myself, "For the baby, for the baby..."

It's morning, and I shoot out of bed way before I have to, familiar taste of bile in my throat. Open my mouth as I lean over the toilet but all that comes out are ropy strings of brown. While I'm dry heaving, Dev stumbles in rubbing his eyes, curls disheveled like Michelangelo's angel torn from the sky. Instead of comforting me that he's near, wish he were in my place, just for a moment.

"You OK?" his voice rough.

"Fine," before puking up some thick greenish stuff.

"Poor Mommy. Do you want some tea and toast?"

Nod, afraid to open my mouth. Close my eyes and lean against the cool tile, taking slow, deep breaths. When I feel close enough to normal, slide up and shake my head.

In the kitchen, food's ready and the chamomile tea works at calming my stomach.

"Whatcha doin' today?" chewing on the slightly burnt crust, pretending normal.

"Practicing the new song. We've got a gig Friday."

"I'll be there if I'm not too tired. Anyway, I'll tell Evelyn today, like I promised."

"Thank you. You know it's for the best."

Wave my hand, cutting off any further conversation. After getting dressed, I kiss Dev on the top of the head then rush out the door. "See you later."

"I'll make dinner."

Take a cab to work, knowing how the conversation with Evelyn will go. Already been on two covers; she's told me so many times over the past few months that I'm her "rising star." Decide to put it off until the end of the shift though, as I have an appointment first thing.

I can tell there's something about this one as soon as he steps out of the elevator. Won't look in my eyes, keeps shifting his weight back and forth on the balls of his feet. Try to pinpoint it, find an excuse not to see him, but I'm being paranoid. All clients are sketchy. Did I think today'd be a breeze because I'm quitting?

"Good afternoon, Eddie. I'm Mistress Averna."

Stares down. "Good afternoon, Mistress."

"Follow me," I say as I lead him into Room One. Don't know why he threw me off like that, he's too sub to even look into my eyes. "What kind of session were you thinking about taking?"

"I want to beat you and then have you punish me for it by beating me."

Pause and breathe, don't sound too annoyed. They love that, to know that they can get the better hand. "I normally don't do switch sessions. How hard are we talking about?"

Eyes dart from his feet to the walls and back to the carpet. "Not very hard at all, I swear, Mistress. Just a few light slaps with a paddle. Five...no, two minutes. I promise."

"If you don't, I will ban you permanently. No second chances. Do you understand me?"

"Yes, ma'am."

"How long were you planning on staying?"

"A half hour?"

"That's fine. I'll take the tribute now."

Looks at me strangely. "I thought I paid you after the session was over?"

"It's customary to do so at the beginning."

"Can you make an exception this time?"

"No." Who does he think he is? Please, please give me an excuse to kick his ass out. No such luck, digs into his pants pocket, counts out the rumpled bills.

Back in the room after handing it over and he's already naked, and hard. "Eager, are we?" I mock, putting the condom on the shelf.

"Can I beat you with this, Mistress?" gesturing toward the bamboo cane.

"How about we start with the paddle?"

"Yes, Mistress, thank you, Mistress." Every nerve is telling me not to let this asshole hit me, but I steel myself. Should have known I'd get the weirdo first thing.

Put my hands against the horse and spread my legs a few inches apart. Body tense, ready to spring at even a hint, but he grazes my ass and upper thighs. After a few strokes, he starts hitting a little harder (sound more than actual pain) and I tell him to stop.

"Time's up. My turn. I'm going to beat you with what you beat me."

"Oh yes, Mistress." Hold out my hand and he gives me the paddle, takes the same stance I did over the horse. "You think you can just beat a mistress and get away with it?"

"No, ma'am."

"At least you're not entirely stupid. Now you're going to pay." Pat him at first, building up; smack him a little more. He jumps up and turns around.

"Hey! What the fuck?" he snarls. "I didn't hit you that hard." Grabs the paddle out of my hand before I know what's happening, followed by darkness.

Know before I open my eyes, from the stale body odor masked with ammonia, that I'm in the hospital. I hate hospitals, would never enter one voluntarily. Last time I was in an emergency room it wasn't even for myself, but when Dev got very drunk, tripped and fell at this little bar in the Village called The Underground. Wound up at St. Vincent's where he got stitches in his shoulder. The whole time I stayed outside smoking, making faces at him through the plate (plexiglas? bulletproof?) window. Even standing outside gave me the creeps.

Turn my head and Dev leaps up and grabs my hand in his, almost knocking over the IV.

"You're awake."

"What happened? Did you let them bring me here?"

"No, I didn't. Your asshole client hit you over the head. Evelyn—is that her name?"

"Yeah."

"Evelyn realized something was up when he ran out and called the cops. They're going to want to talk to you later. Oh, God, Cass. I'm so glad you're awake. You don't know how worried I was."

"I'm fine." Close my eyes, head throbbing, ache carved into the back of my brain. Waves of black zoom and fade into the periphery. Try to remember how it happened when Dev interrupts, "I better go get the doctor." Leaves the room as I squint and check the bracelet on my wrist: St. Vinny's.

A youngish doctor with gold-rimmed glasses walks in behind Dev. First thought is that he's a total sub, could see him get into a little verbal humiliation. Pushes up the glasses on his nose and reads my chart. "How are you feeling, Miss Chambers?"

"Head hurts."

"I imagine that it would. You took quite a knock. I understand that this was a work-related incident?"

Who cares how it happened? So he can laugh along with the rest of them in the staff room? "I got hit in the head with a piece of wood, I think."

"Your charts indicate you suffered a contusion to the back of your head, so that makes sense. I need to check your pupils." Checks my pupils. "They're dilating; that's a good sign." Asks me if I know where I am, what day it is. After I correctly tell him, he says, "Your body seems not to have suffered too much trauma. You had an MRI when we first stabilized you, and there wasn't anything abnormal. We're going to keep you here a night or two to keep track of things, though." Nod, which makes my head hurt even more and I wince.

He turns to Dev, "Are you her husband?"

"Boyfriend."

"Can I speak to you for a moment outside?"

My eyes dart back and forth between Dev and the doctor. "Don't worry, kiddo," Dev smiles. "I'm sure it's no big deal."

"I'll have the nurse come in and give you something for your pain," the doctor says.

"Wait," just realizing. "Is the baby OK?"

Doctor bobs his head in nonresponse before he and Dev walk out. The least he could have done was answer me. What if she's not all right? No, she is. I would have known if she wasn't, I'm her mother.

Nurse comes in and as I'm about to ask, silently shoots my IV with a clear liquid from a syringe. Eyelids immediately get heavy. Dev walks back in, but I can't concentrate on his features. Fight to stay awake and try to ask him what the doctor said, but my jaw doesn't work right and only garbled sounds come out of my mouth. He kisses my forehead as my eyes become lead and I fall asleep.

When I open my eyes again two cops have taken Dev's place.

"Miss Chambers," one says. "We have a few questions related to your assault." (Blatant sneer.) "Can you give us a description of the attacker?"

Can't think right yet, still too sleepy. "I don't know, a little taller than me. He looked like every other client."

"Can't this wait?" Dev asks from the windowsill. "She just woke up."

"Listen," the other one says, "this doesn't rank high on our priority list, youknowwhatI'msayin? Here's my card. Call me for an appointment to come in and look through a few mug shots."

Dark red blooms from Dev's collarbone as he slams his fist on the arm of a chair. "What the fuck? Just because we're not rich means she's not important? What's the name of your supervisor? I'm going to call him."

"Watch your tone, son. And it's Sergeant O'Malley. Call him all you want." They leave the room, chuckling.

Electrical stillness as Dev's color recedes and he gulps a deep breath, holds my hand. "Fuck them. I'm going to call the CCRB in the morning."

"And what good will that do? You heard him. I'm a sex worker. Maybe they would care less if it were a crackhead."

"Maybe they'll make a note in their records or something. Listen babe, you still look really tired. I'm going to go home. I'll call

Alundra and let her know what happened."

He's right, too much going on. Need sleep, need to let my mind and body heal. I'm sure Karen does too. Eyelids drooping...blink open. "What about the baby?" Can't read Dev's face as he kisses my forehead. "Don't worry about it, you're going to be OK, kiddo. I'll see you later."

Too tired to ask him what he means, brain so slow I can only make half-deductions, then back asleep without meaning to.

When I wake up again it's dark and Dev isn't there. Trying to focus my eyes on the clock on the other side of the room. Awhile later a nurse (different from the one before, just as bland) pokes her head in. "Didn't expect to see you up. How are you feeling?"

"I'm OK. What time is it?"

"One-thirty. I need to check your vitals."

As she puts the thermometer under my tongue, I see a ripped piece of notebook paper on the stand next to the bed. "Hi Hon, the nurses made me leave but I'll be there when you wake up. I love you, Dev." She looks into my eyes and takes my blood pressure, while making the appropriate "mmm" noises. "Are you light-headed?"

"Light-headed?"

"Well, you did lose a lot of blood."

Blood? People don't lose blood when they get hit on the head. Then the realization that knocks the breath out of me.

Blank stare as she looks at my face, realizes that I didn't know. "Oh, no. I thought you knew. I'm so sorry." She holds out her arms (to what? Cry to her?), but I put mine up. "I'll be OK," I force out, repressing a primal howl. "Just leave me alone." Why the fuck didn't Dev tell me? Because he's like the rest, trying to wriggle from his responsibilities.

Try to sit up but the pain electrifies and everything gets all swimmy. Can't think, the word "BABY" burning my brain. The nurse doesn't take her eyes off me. "Do you mind leaving me the fuck alone?" She disappears and I can let the hot tears dribble through, punctuated by wet hiccups. Keep rubbing my stomach (why is it still rounded?), hoping they're wrong, that it's a mistake on my chart. How could I not know immediately? It's all a mistake, it has to be. She's still growing in me, she can't be gone. Gotta call Dev, Dev will tell me. I'll know from his voice.

Blinded, I grab the receiver off the tan push-button phone and try to call the house. Rings once. "Hello, Radiology." Slam down the phone, repress a scream and squint at the printed plastic. Pick it up again and dial nine first. Rings three or four times before Dev answers, voice smothered by sleep. "Hello?"

"Fuck you."

"Cassie?"

"Who the fuck else would it be? That was what the doctor was talking to you about, wasn't it? You fucking asshole."

"Aw, shit Cassie, I'm so sorry. I wanted to tell you today but with everything going on I figured you needed to rest first." Pause. "How did you find out?"

"The nurse told me, the fucking nurse. Do you know how that feels, to have a stranger tell me?"

"Babe...I mean, hon, I didn't want you...I'll be there right when visiting hours start."

"Don't fucking bother. How could you not tell me?"

"I know. It killed me not to say something. But they drugged you, and then the cops showed up and I couldn't tell you after that."

"Better that I heard it from the goddamned nurse?"

"I'm sorry, I'm so sorry. I didn't want you to find out this way."

"Whatever. Fuck you." Slam the phone down as hard as I can. No way I'll let this one slide by—this betrayal is too severe. Just like any other fucking man, thinking about himself first.

Rip the stiff cotton sheet from my lap and pull up the gown, expecting to see some bloody trace on my legs, but there's nothing there. What did I do to deserve this?

Just go back to sleep. When I wake up, I'll be at home and tell Dev all about my horrific dream, we'll laugh and he'll help me out of bed, make me tea before he hurries off to work.

Instead, the morning sun is bleaching the white room. Dev's in the molded green chair reading *Rolling Stone*. Stare at him for what seems like forever, sending mental death rays before he finally looks up, smiling tentatively. "Morning, gorgeous. Can I get you anything?"

"Coffee." Hate for him that burns, that it's me who had to go through morning sickness and mood swings, not him. He also didn't share the words I whispered to her in the middle of the night; how much I loved her, how smart she was going to turn out. And now it's me that has to deal with the loss; it wasn't his child, not yet.

"You got it." Playing Ideal Boyfriend, he's back in no time, huge cup in hand. "There you go," putting it on the table beside me. "Didja sleep well last night, after I spoke to you?"

"I guess." Don't tell him about the Technicolor images of black-lipped infants with whips. Feel him watching me as I pick up the thick Styrofoam, blowing across before taking sips, ignoring that it's burning my lips, tongue.

"Listen, Cassie," using his calmest voice (same tone he used on the muggers that held us up while we were cutting through Madison Park two years ago, convincing them to only take the cash) but it enrages me and I hurl the hot liquid at his head. It misses him, landing on the wall behind him, steaming and dripping like an abstract mural.

"How the fuck could you not tell me? How long were you just going to let me keep thinking I was pregnant? You know, I would have realized eventually."

"Cassie, calm down."

"Don't you tell me to calm down."

"I didn't want to freak you out right when you woke. I'm sorry. I wanted to tell you. Do you know how hard it was not to tell you?"

How dare he? "Fuck you, I don't care how you feel."

"I know, you haven't in a long time."

"What's that supposed to mean?" Before I can say anything else, thinking about taking the IV out of my arm and sinking it into his temple, he asks, "How are you feeling?"

Get away from me. "I'm OK."

SEX, BLOOD AND ROCK 'N' ROLL

"How's your head?"

"Not as bad as yesterday. When am I getting out of here?"

"I'll find out." Leaves the room.

Mind is swollen with brackish anger. That asshole killed my baby and he's going to get away with it. Dead baby, dead baby, dead on the floor of a cummed-on carpet. It's not enough that they've taken my sex life, anything but total contempt for the idea of commitment, any chance for a normal life. They had to take my baby as well.

Breathe. Breathe before I rip this shit off me and find him, shove his face in the remains of my child before smashing his skull open with a flogger, slit his balls open with a rusty, AIDS-infected scalpel.

Let this be some mistake. Let the doctor come in and tell me that they mixed up my chart with another Cassie Chambers. That they're very sorry for the confusion and that Karen is as healthy as ever.

Dev and the doctor (different from the one yesterday) come in. "How're you feeling today, Miss Chambers?"

How does he think I feel? "I'd like to go home."

"No one wants to be in the hospital." Chuckles at his stupid quip. "How's the head?"

"It hurts."

"I'm sure it still does. According to the MRI, you have a fairly serious concussion. Also, I'm going to go ahead and schedule you for a D and C. It'll let us know for sure if you'll be able to have children, but I think the chances are good. Normally, it's an outpatient procedure, but given your injury, we want to keep you another night for observation. I don't see why we can't release you in the morning to recuperate at home. I'll be in to check on you later."

He walks out and Dev pulls the chair up close, takes one of my hands in both of his. "That's good news."

Is he dumb and deaf? Did he not hear what the doctor said? Who cares if I can have more children? It's Karen I want. D and C. No, no, can't do that. Can't let them take the rest of her from me, to let my baby become another piece of hazardous waste. Motherfuckers wanted a piece of me and they got it. It's not just one of them, it's all men. Think it's their right to just take. Women are just as bad. Happy to take someone else's lover, or spread rumors for no other reason than their own enjoyment. Humans make me sick. There's no one to trust anymore, if there ever was. Why is Dev looking at me that way? Get out of here.

Door opens again and I'm about to scream for some fucking privacy, but it's another nurse wheeling in a cart with a big bouquet. "These just came for you, and it's time for your medication." Puts the flowers near the phone, takes two blue pills out of a little cup, pours me a cup of water. "Here hon, take these."

Gulp them and only afterward think to say, "What are they?"

"Percosets. Your head will feel better soon. Or rather, your head will still hurt but you won't care," she chuckles as she leaves. They all think they're so funny today.

Dev (seethe that it's me and not him, that he can walk from this, not me, though; I'm scarred) takes the card out of the little envelope.

"'Best wishes for a speedy recovery and we hope to see you soon. Everyone at The Studio.' Too bad you're not going back."

"Who said I was quitting?"

"Cassie, you can't be serious. Look at what happened."

"So? I could've tripped in the stock room at Mike's and cracked my head open."

"I can't believe what you're saying."

"Believe it."

"You get bashed over the head, lose our baby, and you still want to go back?"

He doesn't understand. I have to find the man who did this to me. And if I can't find him, I'll find his moral equivalent. I'll know by looking in their eyes. It was my responsibility, my fuck-up, and I'm going to take care of it. "I'm not arguing this."

Stands up. "You know, there's just no getting through to you sometimes. Even after all this. I need a smoke."

No, I guess there is no getting through to me sometimes. Fuck him. He didn't have morning sickness, didn't feel the baby moving inside him. He didn't get cracked in the head, didn't have to quit smoking, didn't have to feel his skin stretch. So who the fuck is he to tell me anything?

Tears betray again as I remind myself that Karen will never be born. My stomach will not swell until I have to put a hand on my back to stand up. I will never be screaming in agony. Ache in my head and heart not dulled enough by the Percosets. Need to get the fuck out of here.

Dev comes back with a copy of the *Village Voice*. "Here. I thought you could use it to get your mind off things." Looks at his hands before saying, "Cass, I know you've gone through a lot of shit in twenty-four hours, and I don't want to argue with you, but I want you to reconsider going back. Please."

Shut up. With an urge I haven't felt in months, "I want a cigarette."

"Let me go find out if it's all right."

"Fuck if it's all right. Help me to get unplugged and I'll smoke out the window."

"I think they'll notice if the thing that's supposed to track your brain stops beeping."

"It moves." Swing my legs out, head and stomach rushing to catch up, let two windowsills become one again. Lean my body as far out the window as I can with all these tubes in me, flashback of sneaking cigarettes in the girl's bathroom. Tastes as good as it always did and my lungs are still in shock as I take my second drag and the door opens. Hit the back of my neck trying to back out the window.

"Miss Chambers," one of the nurses says. "You know there's no smoking in the hospital."

"Let me go home then."

"Well, I was coming in to tell you that your D and C is scheduled in an hour." To Dev, "Will you be taking care of her when she's released?"

"I'm sorry about this and yes. Her friend will be there when I can't."

"Good. It'll be a few days before she's up and about. And Miss

Chambers, refrain from smoking until you're released."

After the soft thud of the door behind her, "Listen, why don't you go home or something? We're just going to drive each other crazy here."

"You sure? You don't want me here when you get out?"

"No. I'll probably be too out of it anyway."

"You sure you're gonna be OK?"

"Yes, I'll be fine. Just come by to pick me up in the morning."

"OK." Unconvinced, he kisses me on the head. "I'll be here when you wake up tomorrow."

Don't watch him walk out. Pick up the paper, and try to get myself lost in the mayoral scandals the Times won't touch, anything not to think about how soon the remains of my child will be scraped out of me. But the words don't make sense and I put the paper down, then stare out the window.

Nurse returns with an attendant. "Miss Chambers? It's time for your D and C."

"Already?" Defeated, beat. Shouldn't be happening, should be where nothing can hurt me anymore.

They take the tubes out of my arms and scoot me onto the gurney. Shift on the blue plastic, corner where it's cracked sticking into the back of my knee. Exposed; only thing shielding me is the thin hospital gown that doesn't hide much under the florescent lights.

On the way down, everything's careening in snapshots, top of the doorways, broken glass of the inspection sheet in the elevator. No one speaks to me, listen to the nurse tell the orderly about the new coffee place on Seventh.

Room I'm wheeled into is the same tan as the mistress' room in The Studio, with the addition of bland museum posters of watercolor flowers. At first I can only see the tops of the machines (one-legged ghouls), overhead medical lights, scrubbed walls. As they move me into place though, notice the metal instruments neatly lined up (hideous gleam) that will be scraping the remains of Karen.

All turns into an abstract painting as I whip my head around (can't go through with this, no more), trying to not let them see my tears mixing with snot, but there's nowhere to hide; aware of everyone politely turning their eyes away as they prepare.

"We're going to give you a general." Open my mouth, about to say that I'm not feeling anything, but my teeth are too heavy to move.

When I come around, I'm back in the room alone. With a sudden pang, wish I hadn't pretended tough, that Dev were here. Even his face would be better than nothing staring back at me but my thoughts and the coffee-stained wall.

No, it's better this way. He'd just be asking me all these questions, trying to distract me with inconsequential things.

Sore, wishing they could have scraped my mind as well. Look out the window at the gray rooftops of the apartment buildings below me. It's all gone, every trace. Like it never happened at all.

Morning glares, nurse interrupts me as I'm pouring powdered cream into my coffee (shutting up the orderly with a look when he jokes that I need to be more careful with the cup). "We're drawing up the discharge papers now. Perhaps you'd like to call your boyfriend to come get you?"

Phone the house when she leaves but no answer. What the fuck? Calm down, he's on his way, he wouldn't leave me here. Still, where is he? Wondered for awhile if there's a brain under that blond hair; this just proves it. Trying to remember Alundra's number when Dev walks through the door, Associated bag full of clothes in hand.

"How'd you know?"

"I called and spoke to the doctor this morning." Waves the yellow copy of a triplicate form. "You're all set. They even called in your prescription."

"How are we going to pay for this?"

"Sometimes the city ain't so bad. There's a fund set up for the victims of violent sex crimes. They pay for half; the rest we get billed for."

"Really?"

"I wasn't going to argue with them. C'mon, let's get you home."

Check out and exit onto Seventh. Let my eyes adjust to the too bright, hazy sun. "I need a cigarette." Dev hands me one and I inhale, lungs tingling with the overload of chemicals.

"How are you feeling?"

Not looking at him. "Still woozy."

"Well, we'll be home soon. I'll get you all set up."

Find a cab (doesn't want to take us all the way to B, but Dev tells him we aren't getting out until we're at our front door) and as we pull up, opens the door with a hand placed firmly holding my elbow, carrying my bag in the other (relief in the smallest part of my mind, admitting that I do need him, for now). Arm around my waist as he opens the inner door. Shuffle to the foot of the stairs and look up at the wind of metal going up forever.

"We'll take it real slow." And we do, stopping at each landing as I balance my weight between the railing and Dev's arm. Finally, into the apartment, then onto the couch.

"I feel like a fucking invalid."

"You were just in the hospital. Let me make you some soup; you need real food."

"Thank you, yeah." Grab the remote and it's *The Price Is Right*. Watch some fat housewife jump up and down over having won a kitchenette and start thinking about producing my own game show. I'd call it *Circle of Death* and Pammy Polyester would do backflips over having won "Death by Meat Cleaver."

Watching makes me realize how tired I am. Eyelids are attached to weights, everything's warm and it's not long before I'm slipping, crashing, into sleep.

Tristan, the guy Alundra's been talking about, is standing a few feet away from me with his glasses on, wearing olive fatigues and combat boots. Skin is unblemished. He could have walked out of a magazine.

Glide to him, feel myself smile. Smiles back, face alien in its perfection. "Hey. I knew it would be you." Puts his hand on the back of my neck and slides it down my spine, resting on the curve of my back.

Silently turn to leave, knowing he'll follow. When I look behind me to see where we are, it's wavering and shimmery, black with a red door. Crowds pass us, all dressed fabulously but with blank layers of skin where their faces should be.

Turn on what doesn't look like Second Street but has to be because as we walk halfway up the block, there's the small cemetery hidden by a high wall and the heavy boughs of trees. Always locked behind old wrought iron gates in reality, a forgotten afterthought in the post-post-immigration era.

This time the rusty padlock is gone and we slip into the little space. More facelesses walk by, not noticing us under the cover of night. Puts both hands on my upper arms and pulls me to him, low hanging branches brushing against us. Kisses me, his lips so full, begging, as we pull each other onto the ground nestled between graves.

He's on top and unlaces my shirt, freeing my braless breasts, which are dappled with the broken patches of streetlight that shine through the trees. Hands on his back to pull him closer, but not before I see the switchblade on the ground next to us.

Roll over, kissing him as my fingers close around the handle, cold and wet with dew. Move my hand up to caress his fine, strong jawline, then slide the blade under his skin. Doesn't flinch as I finely slit, not breaking away from our kiss.

Sits up and now his glasses are gone. Hands on my thighs, keeping me close to him. Outlining his face in the thinnest trace of crimson, fingers resting on his firm pecs and cherry pit nipples as I slip the metal under, his face coming off like liquid latex, all in one piece. Throw it to the side. He's not bleeding, instead looking like a diagram out of *Gray's Anatomy*. A word from the ragged muscles where his lips used to be. "Yes."

Kiss him again, rooting my tongue in his mouth (absorb his essence), blood rolling over us like fine wine. Pierce each side of him from armpit to the tops of his thighs, lift my skirt and ride him, filling the emptiness as I splay my hand across his chest, kneading the tendons, fucking him harder and deeper than I've ever fucked Dev.

Rising conscious to the low tones of conversation. Alundra's leaning against the kitchen counter, smoking a cigarette and inspecting her chipped nail polish while talking to Dev. Too hazy to catch what he's saying, but sit up when I hear her laugh.

"Hey. I didn't know you were here."

Both turn around and I try to figure out if the look on their faces is a guilty one (what am I saying?).

"Came over a little while ago. How're you doing?"

Shrug. It's all changed now. Can't have her just plop on the couch and tell her everything like I used to. "Better now that I'm home. It's been a long few days."

"I can imagine." You haven't got a clue. "I'm going to baby-sit you tomorrow, so we can catch up then. Gotta run to work now, club opening."

"You sure it's not too early for you to come over?" Dev asks her.

"For you guys, of course not. If I fall asleep, Cassie can kick me if she needs anything. Isn't that right, Cass?"

"Yeah." Uncomfortable silence follows as we glance at one other, small cough from Alundra and then, "I'd better go before it gets too late." Hugs and kisses as I watch how they look at each other. Can't pick up on anything between them, push it out of my head, paranoid (remembering the last time I was paranoid).

Once Alundra leaves, Dev sits on the other end of the couch. "So, how're you really doing?"

"Fine." What am I supposed to say? That we're done, no matter what, that with Karen we lost our last chance? That he could have insisted on a condom like he usually did, to prevent all of this? That I suspect he's making moves on my best friend? Never mind if it's true or not, or if she's even interested. Of course she is—why wouldn't she be? Dev's smart and cute and funny. She's told me so often how she'd kill for someone like him. No—stop this.

"So," as Dev rubs the top of my feet.

"So...I'm not quitting," hoping I sound tougher than I feel.

Blinks before shaking his head. "Whatever, Cass. It's your life."

Empty victory and I roll over; consider sleeping on the couch tonight. Fuck that, I pay half the rent. "Help me into the bedroom." We shuffle in and I position myself at the edge of the bed, as far from him as possible. Too many thoughts crowd my head, pushing each other out of the way. Need to be alone, or as close to it as I can get, even if it's only while I'm asleep.

Dev's already gone when I wake up. Can hear the garbled noises of the morning talk shows Alundra (better be Alundra) has on. Swing both legs off the futon and wince at the dull ache at the base of my skull. Little at a time as I focus on the door and the kitchen counter beyond it, weaving forward for the already made coffee. Alundra looks up.

"You could have called me."

"I can do it myself."

"I know you. Don't you be too proud to ask." Fixes my coffee. "Go sit on the couch."

Lean against the soft, worn-out cushions. Alundra has *Geraldo* on, don't know how she can stand to watch it. "How was work last night?"

"You know, same old. I came home to a message from my mother hysterical about some dream she had about saving me from a burning building. Speaking of, have you told your parents about... everything?"

"We hadn't told them I was pregnant." Last word as a whisper.

A flash (of sympathy? pity? contempt?) crosses Al's face as she nods. "Yeah, I guess they don't need to know about any of it. Here, just how you like it."

Take a sip and smile thanks as we watch the indignant, scantily clad girls trotted out for "My Teen Is Out of Control!" Make fun of the equally trashy mothers. Takes my mind off everything and wait a beat after we're informed who furnished Geraldo's wardrobe before, "Dev's pissed at me for not wanting to leave the dungeon."

"Well, I can't blame him."

Instinct is to tell her that she can fuck off for not seeing my side. Don't, know she's just trying to look out for me.

"Like I told him, I could have gotten hurt anywhere. You remember how I used to have to pick up those huge boxes at the store. What if I tripped on the ladder and landed on my head? Would you both want me to quit there, too?" Gauge her reaction, and then, "Oh, you just don't get it, same as he doesn't."

"No, it's not that, I do. I mean, no, not exactly...no one knows how bad it was but you. But Dev's just looking out for you. We both are."

Stare at my coffee, want to slap the shit out of Al for looking at me that way. Wouldn't be surprised if she and Dev are already sleeping together. No, no—I know she, he, just care, the two who are (were) closest to me.

We've always joked about how whatever Dev couldn't pick up on with me, Al could. No one's made that crack in a while. At first the realization saddens, but that was the old me. As I lay in the hospital, realizing that Karen was really gone, I knew I couldn't quit, certainly not for Dev and Alundra's peace of mind. Plus, I'm good at domination, really good. After the first few fumbles, I took to it (or it to me). Found what I've been searching for my whole life. The surging in my loins as the whip fuses me, the rush at their anguish—it feels right, purity among the unclean, for me to thrash until their skin is swollen, the slight limp as they leave. What would Dev say if I tried to convince him to never play the guitar again? For so long I've been thinking only of others; now it's time to think about myself. If Alundra and Dev (and anyone else) can't adapt to the real me, the one I've become, they can sit and mourn; I won't. Party's over and there's no pleasure in waiting.

Light a smoke. "You're the one who told me to get this job, remember?"

"Don't think I haven't thought about that every second since I found out."

"I'm not quitting."

"All right, suit yourself. But there are plenty of jobs out there. Jobs that won't break up your relationship."

Narrow eyes, dig my nails into my palm. "What are you talking about?"

"I'm your best friend, right?"

Think whatever you want. "Right."

"Well, then listen to me. How long do you think Dev's going to be able to take it, the distance, the sex embargo? It's going to break you guys up sooner or later. Sooner, if you ask me."

I didn't. "He told you this?"

"Not exactly. But between what you told me and what he said last night, it's doesn't take Sherlock Holmes to figure it out."

Now he's telling everyone, spreading our secrets. "What did he say last night?"

"Nothing...well, not a whole lot. That you guys were drifting apart, and that he thinks it's the job. I do too. Asked me if I'd talk to you about quitting."

"And?"

"And I told him I would."

"Great. Both of you are ganging up on me now."

"No Cassie, it's not like that at all. We're trying to look out for you...you haven't been yourself since starting this."

"How have I been different?"

"It's like someone invaded your body." (The real me.) "I'm not telling you this to make you feel bad. I'm telling you this because I'm worried, we're worried." (We're?) "We miss the old Cassie."

Fire in my eyes. "And what was the old Cassie?" The old Cassie was unformed, primer to the masterpiece. Dependent on others, not seeing the truth. Embarrassed to have once been her.

"Happier, more open. This job, it's killing a part of you."

Open a fresh pack and pull out a cigarette. "Maybe I'm happier this way. Maybe I wanted that part to be dead." Alundra's jaw actually drops a little, then she goes back to watching TV.

Yeah, chew on that, as I pick at some fuzzies on the couch. Hilarious that she's telling me what to do with my life. She, whose longest relationship lasted four months. Alundra loves to play at being worldly, but she's in just as much of a box as all the rest. Try to remember why we were ever friends at all.

She waits until a commercial before saying, "What about a shrink? You've been through an awful lot lately. Maybe it'll do you some good."

"There's nothing wrong with me." To prove my point, reach behind and grab the phone, punching the numbers with purpose.

"Good afternoon."

"Hi Evelyn, it's Averna."

"Averna, darling, how are you?"

"I'm better. Came home from the hospital yesterday."

"Wonderful. I take it that means you're on the mend?"

"Starting to feel better."

"Well, I don't have to say that there's always a place for you here. I was going to call you in a few days, but now that you're on the phone," voice drops, "I was speaking to our lawyers. I don't know if you were thinking about pursuing legal remedies but as you didn't sign a waiver, we are fully prepared to acknowledge full liability on this issue." Click of her lighter followed by raspy smoker's inhale. "We're willing to give you twelve thousand for your doctor bills as well as for pain and suffering."

Twelve grand? No fucking way. I'm about to ask her to repeat that and then realize she doesn't know the medical bills were partly paid for. If she's offering that much, wonder how much I could get if I sued her, how much she's worth. Bet I could get at least double, but then I'd have to go through the trouble of actually going to court. "I'm not sure. I have to think about it, maybe talk to a lawyer." Alundra's giving me her "what are you talking about?" face.

"Of course, of course. I hope you know that whatever you decide, we'd like to have you back when you're ready."

"Thank you."

"When do you think you'll be able to return? If you want to, of course."

"I'm not sure. It depends on what the doctors say. A week and a half, two weeks maybe."

"Just let us know, there's always room. The clients are very eager to see you again."

"What was that all about?" Alundra asks after I hang up.

"Nothing. Lawyers." Money's none of her business; if I tell her, she'll tell Dev.

"Cass, I didn't want to piss you off with what I said earlier."

"I know," as I go back to pretending to watch whatever crap is on TV. No, won't tell Dev—all he'll do is try and take some of it from me. Good thing that we never followed through on our half-assed plan to combine bank accounts.

Twelve and three zeros, more than I've ever seen in one place. Already spending it in my head. Move out, of course, as soon as I'm better. What about the rest? First thought is to blow the rest in Barcelona, maybe invest? Then, an idea flickers—my own dungeon. I've learned all I can from The Studio, no reason to stay there. Evelyn's just a pimp, taking half my money. Most mistresses are independent anyway and my regulars would keep me afloat. Even with just a few quarter page ads, I'd make my money back and then some in a few months. Maybe something can come out of this debris. A gateway, my cobblestone path to freedom.

So she can't tell what I'm thinking about, act normal and feign enough interest that Alundra tells me about her dates with Tristan (he's pushing to get more serious, she doesn't know if she can handle dating only one guy). Watching her mouth move like a fish, dawns on me that she's no different from most of the friends I had in Priory before Spike and Marcus, only with cooler clothes and dyed hair. The thought strikes me as so funny that I'm giggling uncontrollably (Alundra thinks it's her description of an ex-boyfriend's ex-girlfriend) when Dev walks through the door with grocery bags.

"How's my girl?" Kisses me on the cheek.

"Much better. Alundra's taking good care of me."

"Thanks for doing this, Al."

She waves him off. "That's what I'm here for." Takes her bags from the floor.

"You're not leaving, are you?" he asks.

"I need some sleep. See you guys tomorrow."

Dev closes the door behind her and there's this long moment of silence as we look at each other, him trying to plead with his eyes. Instead of being touched like I used to (so hard to remember that time), all I can think now is how pathetic. He doesn't want to break up, what's wrong with him? Not that stupid, or masochistic, is he? Perhaps it's habit, the devil you know and all that. Still, there's no reason why we should be together. Used to think love would bind us, but that's a joke. Need more than that now, and he can't give it to me. If I were to tell him all this, it would draw things out unnecessarily, pleading with me that he can be whatever I want to him to, etc. He can't stop being who he is and I can't stop being who I am.

Instead of screaming my thoughts, I light a cigarette, pretending that the tension is getting to me too, staring at my cuticles as Dev puts the groceries away, slamming the cans in the cabinet, closing the fridge door harder than needed. Soon enough, I want to tell him, we'll be out of each other's hair for good.

Call The Studio first day I don't need Alundra, tell Evelyn I've spoken to my lawyer, that it's in my best interest to take the settlement. It's ready for me, she says, I can come over whenever I want. Funny how she knew that I was going to take the check.

Get dressed slowly to prevent the dizzy spells that are still lagging and take a cab. No angst, nothing unusual until the elevator opens into the waiting room. Return to the nausea of that morning. Chest seizes and I want to gag, but Evelyn's standing by the office's open door; swallow it down.

"Averna," holding her arms out. "I'm so glad to see how well you're doing." Smile as if I believe her and walk into the office, sit down as she closes the door behind us.

"So," as she pulls out an expensive cream envelope with the cursive lettering of a law firm in the corner. "Do you think you'll be coming back to us?"

"I'd like to."

"Wonderful. When can we expect you?"

"I'm almost all better. Need a few more days to make sure I can get around on heels."

"Take your time, there will be plenty of clients. I've installed intercoms in each room so you girls can call out if there's a problem."

"Hopefully it won't happen again."

Small cough. "Yes, well."

Stand up. "I should be going," and she walks me to the elevator.

"I mean that, you know, about having you back," as the door slides closed.

Car hasn't moved before I open the envelope and blink at "Twelve thousand," written in elegant fountain pen from the escrow account of Dylan, Smith and Greene.

Go to the bank, deposit the check (rather cash it and keep it stored in my drawer where most of my pay is, but can't risk Dev seeing it).

Going to walk home, but feel woozy after a few blocks, take a cab the rest of the way.

Phone's ringing as I'm walking up the stairs. "Hello?"

"You're alive." Dev.

"Of course I'm alive. Why wouldn't I be?"

"Because the phone just kept ringing and ringing. Where were you, anyway?"

"Walked up to the park and read. Needed some fresh air."

"Oh. Wish you would have told me first."

"What? Now I have to check in? When did you become my father?"

"No, I didn't mean it like that."

"Whatever. I'm gonna go lie down." Hang up before he can ask how I'm feeling. His voice, once so smooth, now grates in its passivity.

Make myself some coffee, scan the real estate section of the *Voice*. Doing quick figures in my head, I know I can only afford one space to live and work for now. Better anyway, to make the jump quickly and never come back.

Indulge in the last days of luxury, of not having to do anything, knowing it won't be this way again for a while. Dev mistakes this for me changing back. Want to laugh in his naive, pretty-boy face.

Don't tell him that I'm going back to The Studio until the night before, as I'm wrapping up the remains of the fake crabmeat and cheese not-quite casserole he made. Bangs his hand on the table and glares, but stands down when I look at him, then goes onto the fire escape for a beer and smoke. Later stands over me with arms crossed as he watches me pack my latex stockings and new leather dress. Is this supposed to deter me?

"Cassie, we need to talk about this."

"There's nothing to talk about."

"Don't you see what this is doing to us?"

"No Dev, doing to you. It's your problem. You have to deal." Stunned, walks out, probably to The Mission. Comes home late, feel him bump in bed, stroke me once before moving to his side.

The next morning (day's already started well, Dev at work when I wake up) I jump out of bed with only one thought—I have to find him, the asshole (whose real name I don't even know); reciprocate the pain.

Get to The Studio (can't crack here, they don't deserve it). Knock, open the door to the office. "I'm back."

"What a wonderful sight. It was so empty without you. You look better than before, if that's possible. I booked some of your regulars so you have a full schedule for the next few days."

"Guess I should get changed then."

"You go do that. I'm sure the girls are anxious to see you."

Into the room, where Sybille, Victoria and Paige are dressing. When I close the door behind me, Sybille looks up from lacing her leather miniskirt and runs over.

"Hi! How're you feeling? Did you get the flowers? We were all going to come visit you, but you were out so quickly."

"It's cool. I was up and about in no time anyway."

"Well," Paige says, lighting a cigarette. "You look great. We missed you."

Victoria actually stops powdering her face and forces a "Yes, welcome back."

Unpack and change into the black embroidered bustier and matching skirt I picked up at Religious Sex. Sybille stares as I brush my hair. "I don't know what it is about you, but you look different."

I got hit in the head and lost my baby? "Changed my hair color?"

"Yeah, maybe that's it."

Evelyn opens the door. "Averna, Harry Four is coming in soon. Victoria, John Eight will be here in a half hour."

Harry Four...Harry Four. "Evelyn, who is this guy again?"

"Tall, glasses. Likes the St. Andrew's Cross."

Rolodex my mind until it stops on Harry Four. Seen him five or six times; bondage, humiliation, dildo training (like saying I'm the goth with long, dark hair).

Buzzer rings and I bounce off the couch arm, reaching the elevator door before it opens. Stepping out is an extremely eager-looking Harry Four.

"I'm so glad to see you back, Mistress. I trust you had a good vacation. I brought you flowers in anticipation of seeing you, ma'am. Is that acceptable?"

"Yes, Harry, it is," lead him to Room Two, take the tribute. "I'll be right back." Walk down the hall while smelling the darkened roses. (Gotten the occasional gift from clients—shoes, a garter belt or two, real silk stockings that they want me to wear in session.

Only thing I couldn't resist bringing home were these thigh-high stilettos with silk ribbon up the front that looked too good to be wasted on these assholes.)

Back in with equipment, Harry's kneeling naked by the Cross. Lifelong bachelor, awkward in his movements, same haircut (and wardrobe) since the sixth grade. Staring at his back. Want to mark it, make my own. For the first time, see not the moles or birthmarks on the curve of his shoulder blades as his head is bowed obediently, but the brilliance of his vulnerable flesh, the dip in his spine, vertebrae piecing themselves together, flaunting themselves at me as they connect with his skull. Even the slight love handles over his hips that yesterday I would have been disgusted at enthrall me today.

"What a good boy. All ready for me."

Shakes his head but doesn't turn. "Yes, ma'am."

Trace my nails with just enough pressure to make him jerk. "I knew I liked you. You may be my most well-behaved slave." Sits still as he tries not to beam—knows my punishment for talking out of turn. As his muscles tighten, instead of figuring out how to shave moments off the session, find myself hoping he'll want to extend the hour. Eager to dole out pain, yearning stronger than sex.

Grab the hair at the top of his neck hard and force-walk him to the Cross, push him against it. "Stay right there. Don't move, don't turn your head." Pull out bundles of rope from the drawers, and run the cords around, tying tight around the wrists and ankles, shoulder blades almost meeting. "Nice," and we haven't even started yet.

Lift the bamboo cane. Tested it on the side of my thigh in

between sessions early on, when I was still learning everything. Split second of nothing and as soon as the thought "it doesn't hurt so bad," nerves caught up with the pain receptors and screamed along the perfect red stripe that hurt for the rest of my shift.

"Are you happy, slave? Is this where you want to be?" Bring my arm down, air making the sharp cracking sound. Harry stiffens. "Do you know what that is, slave? You may speak."

Carefully, as if he doesn't want to be wrong about this, "Yes, I think so."

Crouch behind him and breathe on the back of his neck, "I think you know, too." Stand and trace the wood up his neck, raise my arm like a conductor, then bring it down. Electricity flows through the wood and back into me as his muscles tighten, involuntarily defending when he feels the whoosh yet again as I rip the cane through the air. Not noticing or caring if I'm hitting the same spot twice, the top of his ass and the side of his legs marked over and over, tiny triangles of white between broken capillaries.

"How are you doing, slave?"

"Oh, wonderful, Mistress. Thank you, Mistress," voice gasping through tears.

Next: paddle or crop? Crop. Run my hands down his back and sides of thighs, pressing hard against the swelling welts so he winces.

"Please be gentle," he says, no longer role-playing.

"Of course, my pet," landing three in quick succession on the raise of his ass. Pause to let his pain sink to the root. I could just keep hitting and hitting until red's weeping through the skin and he's crying blood. Squashed by too much emotion, force myself to break away and take a breath. Calm, calm. Stay here, don't get carried away. Lay the cane down and blow lightly across his shoulders, down his back.

"I think you've had enough punishment. Good boy. You deserve your reward now." Untie one of his wrists and toss him the condom. Strap myself in, lube up. Fingertips across his upper arm, down his back, inhaling the pre-sex anticipation; gloved hand across his bruised ass, leaving traces of lube in his hair.

Slather on more K-Y, push in the head a little. Slightest resistance of sphincter, start to fuck him, feel his asshole constricting on my cock. Push in and out until his hips aren't even moving anymore, and he's just lying there (meat). Fucking and fucking, nothing else in the world exists.

Hold onto his shoulder for leverage, fingertips barely an inch from his neck. How stupid to be this exposed to someone you don't know. Breath catches as I realize how easily I could squeeze. To feel his life pass through me, as easy as blowing out a candle (as easy as miscarrying a child). Crisp mental image of finger joints around his windpipe releases a wetness I haven't felt in the longest, wouldn't be surprised if it was running down my leg, making a puddle on the floor. Only so much one person can take before it boils over.

Squeeze imperceptibly, but then he turns his head and just like in my fantasies, I stop before culmination. In his mind, death's the least of his worries and he finishes. Light-headed, dizzy as I pull out. He gets dressed and I clean up, but I'm far away. So close, could have.

Not sure who's wobbling more as I walk him out. Other two sessions of the day ("Thought I'd start you slow," Evelyn tells me when I ask why so few) are mindless enough (cross-dresser who wants to be told how pretty he is, how to sit like a lady; and the Paddler), while I replay every second of the texture of Harry's neck under my fingers, speeding up at some points, slowing in others. Except in my mind, I crush his windpipe; crunch of trachea as his head lolls forward.

A week or so later I'm sitting at the edge of the bed painting my toenails red when Dev comes home and stands in the doorway for a moment, watching me before putting his stuff down.

"What?"

"Nothing. How was your day?"

"Fine." In earlier times, would have told him to cut the shit out but now it would open Pandora's box.

Manage to avoid him until I'm heading to bed, when he looks up from reading (when was the last time *he* read a book?). "Since you're feeling better, I'm going out after work tomorrow. Having a few drinks with the guys."

Not because of the statement—we used to go out separately all the time—but because he announced it, I consider following him, to catch him in the act of nuzzling the sweaty neck of one of his little fans, or Alundra in the basement of the Continental. How I could turn the tables and shove it all down his throat.

Stop. Let him do what he wants (maybe it's that little redhead who's always by the front of the stage taking pictures).

"What are you going to do?" he asks.

"I dunno. Maybe go out myself."

Scarfing down a ham and cheese during a thirty-minute break between sessions, greasy mayo at the corner of my mouth, when Sybille comes in, lights a smoke.

"I don't know how you can eat that and not get fat."

"I walk a lot. You doing anything after work?"

"A bunch of us are going to this new bar, Meow Mix. You up for it? Supposed to have decent music."

Meow Mix, Meow Mix—why does that name sound familiar? Then I remember that we've passed by it on our way to The Bank. Used to be the Far Side, now a lesbian bar. Dev's probably going out to get laid and who the fuck cares what he thinks anyway.

"Sure, when?"

"Around midnight."

"I didn't know you were into girls. Weren't you dating Slug?"

"That was ages ago, and working in the business...you become less and less enthralled with the penis, you know?" Yes, I do. "Anyway, I guess if some guy was really hot, I'd go for it. Don't know anyone in the business who doesn't dabble, at least occasionally."

Home after my shift, relaxed at the knowledge that Dev's out, won't be breaking my tranquility. After a short nap, wake up feeling refreshed; shower, then decide on my boots, tight jeans and bra top with pinstripe vest.

Soft wind tickling my neck as I walk up to A. Though it's only been a few weeks, getting harder to restrain myself. A few days ago, one of my regulars, Jeff Seven, came in for his noon appointment. An accountant, very exact. Will only use Room One, schoolboy fantasy. Likes the paddle, wants me to humiliate him for peeking up girl's skirts during recess, "Just wait until your mother finds out." Call him dirty while he finishes off, no deviation.

When the door opened, I could tell it wouldn't be the usual easy hundred. First words out of his mouth were: "Where are the stockings you normally have on?" When I see Jeff, I always wear the black thigh-highs with the seam up the back. Forgot that day. "You're right. If you like I can change into them."

"No time. We'll just have to make do."

Didn't let myself get irritated, not his fault I forgot. But he had to point it out, didn't he? He couldn't have thought that maybe I have other concerns, maybe there are more important things than if I remembered the fucking stockings with the seam. So typical—as if my whole world revolved him.

Could feel my blood pressure rise as I lifted the fraternity paddle, nicks in the heavy lacquer. "Sister Margaret told me she caught you on the playground." Hands folded neatly behind his back, wanted to shove his smarmy thoughts through the back of his brain, matter splattering over the mirror like a gunshot.

Didn't know if he saw it in my eyes when I said, "You'll need to be spanked for that," but he felt it when I brought the paddle down with all my strength, throwing him off his elbows before he had time to brace; face on the carpet.

"Hey," putting his glasses back on. "That's not the way it's supposed to go."

"I'm sorry, I thought that a dirty boy like you could take your punishment."

"Yes, yes, ma'am."

"Tell me what you did. I want to hear it from your mouth."

"I was looking up a girl's skirt."

"And why were you doing that?"

"To see what was underneath."

"What did you see?"

"I saw panties." Erection growing.

"What color were those panties?" Wonder if he really does this, or is it just his imagination? Either way, he pictures little girls (Karen) while he comes here trying to absolve his guilt.

"White."

"Fucking pervert," raise my arm, hit him harder than I did before because I wanted to bring innocence into this world and these scumbags want to feed off that.

"Wait, hold on..."

Didn't answer, hit him harder; only thought was of beating the fantasies out of him.

"Enough, enough."

"No, not enough," ready to smack him again to purify both him and myself—seeing him curled in a ball, bleeding from his nose, his ears, gore dripping from the gash on his thinning scalp.

But before I could carve him, Evelyn burst through the door.

"Averna, what are you doing?! Jeff, please accept my apologies. I don't know what could have gotten into her. If there's anything we can do to make it up to you..."

"No, that won't be necessary."

"At least let us refund your session."

"I'd prefer to leave. Rest assured I'll be taking my business elsewhere."

"I want to see you in my office," Evelyn fumed at me before walking Jeff to the elevator.

Kicked off my heels before opening the office door. Without looking up from her paperwork, Evelyn snapped, "What has gotten into you? He was a regular, your regular. I understand that it hasn't been easy, but this is inexcusable."

"I'm sorry," that I was interrupted.

"I'm not going to dock you, considering what you've been through, but this is a warning. If you continue to drive customers away, it may be time for a break." Nod as if I'm listening. "You don't have any other appointments today. Take the rest of the shift off. Get a drink; there's a great lounge that opened down the block. Their apple martinis are fabulous."

"Thanks, maybe I will."

Smile at the recollection as I walk past the kids playing ball in the street, running back to the curb when someone drives down the block, then charging out into the street to make the cars stop short; past the hard-core junkies who've underestimated their stash looking to cop this late. Quick to East Houston, past buildings alternatively condemned and sparkling; neon sign for Katz's

SEX, BLOOD AND ROCK 'N' ROLL

Deli a few blocks up, fading ghosts of generations of immigrants crowding into tenements coming to the New World with the gold-threaded fantasy of making their lives, and their children's lives, better. Not realizing it's the same wherever they go.

Meow Mix is down the block, and I race across the six-lane street to reach the bar's dark blue door. Woman in baggy jeans and a cap takes my five bucks, stamps my hand.

Inside, didn't do much renovating. Stage still takes up half the place; bar along the back wall lit with red Christmas lights and vintage signs for Rheingold and Pabst, stickers taking every available space on the mirror.

Place is full, on the border of being uncomfortable; bartender in chic cowgirl dyke (tank top and blue jeans), short auburn hair on a cheekboned face. Wedge in, order a rum and coke. Take a sip and turn. No different from any other bar. Good mix, guys who are there careful not to make eye contact. Don't see Sybille (no, Lila here) but catch someone else by the window. Shoulder-length brown hair, big eyes, curves. No Brixton, but still easy on the eyes. Low-cut black T-shirt and a silver chain resting between her breasts. She's doing the same look-around, notices me boring a hole into her. Stares as she leans back, both elbows on the sill. Bites her lip and looks coyly at me again, then away.

Doesn't take her eyes off me as I shoulder through people, stopping short when I'm close enough to see she's not nearly as cute as she appeared from across the room. Break eye contact looking for an escape, shove through the crowd to get to the stairs near the front door that lead to the basement.

Find Lila and Cleo playing pool with two other girls, one looking like a hotter version of Neve Campbell—carnival tattooed sleeves, nose and lip rings reflecting the little light coming off the low-hanging lightbulbs, slashed, old Ramones T-shirt showing off her flat stomach.

"Hey," Lila kisses me on the cheek as Cleo waves from where she's leaning against the wall. "This is Susan and the one chalking her cue is Lindsey." Both smile; Lindsey's a little butchier, crewcut, wearing a wifebeater. "Wanna play next, Cass? I'm almost done kicking Lindsey's ass."

"That was just my warm-up game. Next match, you'd better watch it, girl."

"Uh-huh," as she sinks the eight ball. Walk over to Cleo. In my ear, quiet but close enough so I can hear her breathe over the music, "How're you doing? You know, now that you're back and all."

"Good. I thought it would take time to get back into things, but it was easier than I thought it would be."

"I thought you were going to quit after that, not like anyone could blame you, but I'm glad to see you again. We all are."

Laugh. "Even Victoria?"

"Well, maybe not her."

Susan walks over. "So, you work with them?"

Hoping it's not just idle conversation. "For a few months now."

"Do you like it?" Body language—one long leg toward me, leaning forward. Turn so I open myself, chest up.

"Yeah, I like it." Grin wide. "I mean, I do get to beat up men for a living." Laughs, twirls her hair and I've got her.

Mirror her gestures as we chat. Doesn't take a brain surgeon to know that to get a girl in bed, only have to pretend to care about what she's saying (used to fall for it all the time before I realized). Appropriate nods as she tells me she works as a bartender at Doc Holliday's over on A, plays bass in one of the local grrrl groups, Pixie Dust. Wet eyes twinkling, looking right into mine.

Break from her gaze when the ice from the drink bangs against my teeth. Smile, then go back upstairs, to get another for me, a cider for Susan. Beautiful From Afar is now sitting at the bar alone, staring (glaring?) at me as I order.

Labyrinth back downstairs, hand Susan the can. "You read my mind."

"I'm good like that."

Keeps talking as I convince her I care with my rapt silence. Finally, "Wanna come with me to pee?"

"Sure."

Takes my hand firmly in hers, leads me to the bathroom behind the stage, my eyes on her firm ass the whole way. Soon as she slides the lock behind us, takes my face in both her hands, kisses me hard. "I've been waiting to do that all night."

Lean in, my turn to push her against the wall. "Wait, I really do have to pee," she says as she squats over the toilet. As she's pulling up her pants, grab her with zipper down and open her mouth with mine, slide my tongue in. Working lips open, thick sweetness. Hand on her shoulder, another on (new) hips. Drooling, pulling at each other's shirts, skin.

Broken up by someone banging on the door. Susan giggles, pulls away. "We'd better get back downstairs, anyway. They're gonna think we disappeared."

"Who cares?" as we leave, past the long line that's snaked.

Everyone else is by the stairs, finishing their drinks. "We didn't think you guys were coming back," Lila says. "It's getting late, I gotta go soon."

Look down at my watch, and oh shit—how'd it get to be three already? "I'd better be going, too. Have a lot to do tomorrow."

Susan grabs a flyer for some shitty band's gig at Brownie's, scribbles her number down, tears the flyer in half, gives me her pen. "Here, give me yours." Hesitate and she says, "I should have asked you before if you were with someone."

"No, no," touch her sweat-moistened shoulder. "I'm...I'm just getting out of something."

"Oh. Boy or girl?"

"Boy."

"Don't worry about it then. Just tell him I'm a friend from work."

She's got a point, as I pen my digits, then one more groping kiss before I run across Houston.

My footsteps are too loud on the cracked marble steps leading to the apartment. Fumble with the keys (must be drunker than I thought) and inside Dev's laying on the couch, watching *It Came from Outer Space*.

"I was getting worried about you," as I lock the door behind me.

"I'm fine. I told you I was going out. And besides, weren't you supposed to be out with the guys?"

"I was still getting worried." Gets up, reaches his hand toward me but I step back, not wanting his stain.

"I told you, I'm fine. God, when did you become my mother?"

Takes a step back, hurt radiating, and for the first time I don't feel even the smallest smudge of regret, apathy or even impatience. Satisfaction spreads through me like a shot of good whiskey. Leave him like that and head into the bedroom, stripping to my underwear before sliding in, room threatening to revolve.

Two Devs stand in the doorway. "You know, Cassie, we really have to talk."

Don't move. "Cass, I know you're still awake."

"Yes, alright," before turning away.

In the morning, open the real estate section of the *Voice* and roll a joint, blowing the pot dust onto the floor. Budget with my shitty math; approximating advertising, equipment, space. It'll be tight but I can manage.

Spend the rest of the day in the West Village getting supplies; a cell phone to fit my "active lifestyle"; business cards from Village Copier chosen under the harsh florescent lights (pick glossy black with red curly lettering—just "Averna" and my cell number).

Done, stroll back to St. Mark's instead of straight home and slip into Bull McCabe's unnoticed (block is weirdly empty of recognizable faces—something going on I don't know about?). Bull McCabe's is a classic old-man whiskey bar straight out of a movie, with uncomfortable wood stools and a TV in the corner silently showing the game. Propped against a wall in the back beer garden is half an airplane—rumor is it belongs the owner, who crashed and put it in the back as a reminder of how precious life is.

Sit down and order a screwdriver. A few regulars sit in a clutch at the end of the bar, one of them waving his hands and ranting about "that bitch," while the others nod their heads in silent solidarity. Near them are some bland souls who could be wallpaper. Two bikers feed the jukebox. Stop myself from laughing out loud at how insignificant they all are. Guy over there sipping his drink—how is his life precious (more so than Karen's)? All these men, these scumfucks...they want nothing more than to hurt the women who love them. Not that women are any better—suckers for not seeing what's in front of them, for being so fucking weak that they let these assholes in. I, on the other hand, was put on this earth for a higher purpose. S&M's just a stepping-stone. Feeling warms me (or is it the vodka?).

In the midst of my musing, sense someone sitting next to me. Turn and glare. Looks like Jesus, probably an artist. Once, in my other life, might have thought him cute.

Gives me a laid-back smile. "Hey, what are you drinking?" with the brash confidence of getting laid a lot.

"Screwdriver," angry at being interrupted.

"Yeah? I'm drinking a beer."

"I can see that." If life imitated art (fantasy), I'd drag him back to the apartment, fuck him, then slash open his pretty face.

Looks around, pretending to search for something to say. "So, uh, I didn't catch your name."

"Tamara."

"Hi Tamara, I'm Griffin. You know," crooked smile, "like the mythical beast."

"I know."

"So Tamara, you do coke?"

Even if he had more than Tony Montana, I have no patience for this. "I'd like to be alone, OK?"

"Aw, come on. Your day couldn't have been that bad."

"I'm asking you politely to leave me alone."

Tries his most charming smile. "You don't mean that."

Stand and slam my open palm against the thinly varnished wood, lean over him. "I told you to fuck off." With red seeping in my sight and hands not my own, hold his shoulder and punch him right in the jaw. Then, not even thinking, begin hitting; whole point of my existence is to beat him to a pulp. Don't even feel it when I cut my knuckles on his teeth. Jolted when the bartender, a teddy-bear tough grizzly blues man named James, grabs my arm.

"Enough. He got the point. You'd better get out of here."

A circle's formed around us and I step back. That was far too good. Scared of myself, I look down at my would-be suitor. Blood (much darker than one would think) streaming down his face, cheekbones a mess, nose a memory. Yeah, I'd better go.

Rinsing off my knuckles in the bathroom sink (Dev looks up from working on chords but decides better than to ask) when the phone rings.

"Hello?"

"It's me. How've you been? I haven't spoken to you in ages."

"Who-oh, hi Al. I know. I've been...busy."

"Yeah, I heard. So, what have you been up to?"

"Not much. You know."

"That's not what Dev said when I called for you earlier."

"Yeah?"

"He started talking about you immediately. I mean, he was almost in tears. I wouldn't have mentioned it if it weren't for that."

Light a Camel and almost bite through the filter, dig my nails into my palm. "What else did he say?"

"He doesn't want to break up with you, but you're too far gone. You're not yourself, Cass. I'm begging you. You've gotta at least talk, let him in."

"Or?"

"Or he's gonna leave. And I will, too."

"And I'm sure that will fit in with your plan just perfectly."

"What the hell are you talking about?"

"I'm talking about how you've wanted Dev since the day you met him. Well, now's your perfect chance."

"Oh God, Cass. You're out of your mind."

"No? How many times did you tell me you'd love to have Dev as your boyfriend? How incredible he is?"

"I never meant it like that. I can't believe you'd actually think this."

"Why? Because it's true?"

"Maybe it would be best if you and Dev broke up. What's gotten into you?"

"The truth. I should have known it all along." Slam down the phone. Face contorts as I go back to the front and knock Dev's notebook off the table.

Snaps his head up. "What the fuck is wrong with you?"

"What did you tell Alundra?"

"Cass, I didn't know what to do, I had to talk. I can't take it anymore."

Light a smoke. "I would appreciate it if you would not spread our life all over the place."

He swallows hard. "Maybe we should spend some time apart. I'm going to sleep on the couch tonight."

"Yeah, maybe you should."

Doesn't take me long to find a place. Partly converted loft on Gansevoort in the Meatpacking District, not far from Mother's.

"It's a mess, lady," the super tells me. "And you know the neighborhood. But it's big and cheap."

Ignore him as I look around. Open room as you walk in, high factory ceilings, all painted impersonal white, windows high on the wall. Already imagining what would go where. Doorway in the middle of the right side leads into a smallish kitchen, bath, and another room that could easily fit my stuff.

"I'll take it."

Surprise crosses his face as he takes the toothpick out of his mouth. "Really? I mean, that's great. Is your boyfriend going to be living here, too?"

"I don't have a boyfriend."

"Oh," he says, I'm sure picturing lesbian oil wrestling. "I'll call the landlord now. Here's his card. Give him a ring later on today."

Come back from dropping off the first month's rent and security at an office on the outer edge of Thirty-Eighth with bulletproof windows and an uninterested secretary chewing gum, sliding the fill-in-the-blank lease through a slot only big enough to push papers through. Go home, find the tattered phone book, call movers, find one willing to move me late afternoon tomorrow, when Dev has band practice.

Don't want to look at him when he comes home, closing the bedroom door when I hear his key in the lock. Bumps around for a few minutes, close of the refrigerator door and then the tentative chords of a new song.

Swing open the door when I hear him playing the usual A-G combination. He doesn't look up. I could let it go, as anticlimactic at that would be. One last dig instead. "Nice tune."

"I didn't know you were here."

"Where else would I be?"

"Come here, will you? We need to talk. Now. I'm not sleeping another night on the couch. Either we decide to work this out or one of us has to go."

Mouth twists into a grin as I'm about to giggle, but then stop. Instead, sit on the couch, put my hand on his. "I know."

"Cass, I love you, I miss you."

"So do I." If I make him believe, tomorrow will be that much worse for him. "I've been doing a lot of thinking and...you're right. I want the old us back, too. I decided to quit mistressing."

"Really?"

"It's not worth the money. I love you." Getting harder to keep from laughing.

"Oh Cass, I'm so relieved. I thought you were getting ready to leave. I know so much has gone down, but I don't know what I would have done without you." Hugs me. So desperate he can't see through my crocodile tears. Deserves what he's getting.

Kisses the side of my neck and I get rigid; thought of touching him, of letting him touch me, nauseating. Lean back, "I'm not ready yet."

"Why not? It's been awhile, Cass."

Can't go through with it without ruining the joke. "I'm not feeling very well, tired. That's what I was doing in the bedroom—lying down."

"I understand. Why don't you go back to sleep. I'll be in later."

"You're so good to me." Kiss on the cheek. "Good night."

Into bed chuckling, wishing I could be a fly on the wall tomorrow. Not tired, but I squeeze my eyes closed, force myself to sleep so I won't have to feel him next to me.

Next morning, after Dev closes the door behind him, garbage bags and tape come from under the bed. All of it goes with me—clothes, pots and pans his parents gave us for Christmas, shampoos, linens, coffeemaker, silverware, record player that was Dev's long before I came along. Even take the phone, so he'll have to go to the corner to make a call.

Why not take it all? Dev, for his pretty face and graceful words, is no better than the one who hit me over the head. Saying all those things to control me, to keep me like the others. He loves himself, his cock and his music. In that order. Only reason he didn't fuck all his little groupies in their bra-tops was that I was a fixture at his shows. That's the only thing that stopped the adorable brunette with perfect curls last time he played at the Continental, giggling and gazing at Dev's one-word answers as he had his after-show cigarette.

Movers come when I'm about half-finished. Takes less than an hour, two big guys carrying the bags down, a little harder to manage the dresser, the futon, TV, couch. They chuckle when I dump Dev's stuff in a pile on the floor.

Leave a note where the coffeemaker used to be. "Had to go, changed my mind. It's not working. I'll see you around."

Takes only two trips in the freight elevator to get all my stuff into the new place. Spend the rest of the day and the next slowly setting up, listening to The Dictators (on Dev's stereo, think with some glee). All my not-for-the-business stuff fits nicely in the small living area in the back.

When I'm done, front room is simple and sparse, with cat-o'-nines, bamboo cane, riding crops and, of course, dildos; get a stainless steel rack on which to hang it all from a restaurant supply place on the Bowery. Wandering around Chelsea one day after work, come across an ebony lacquer bookcase with doors, perfect to hold the other toys. Too hard to find a ready-made St. Andrew's Cross, wind up buying the wood and O-rings myself, painting it black before nailing it up with huge spikes to the wall. Martha Stewart would be proud.

At The Studio, let my regulars know I'm leaving, all of them congratulating me and promising to call as I slip them my card before walking them to the elevator.

On what I decide will be my last day, hand Sybille my cell number on a scrap of paper. "I'm quitting today."

"Where are you going?"

"Out on my own."

"Holy shit. Does Evelyn know? No? Shit girl, she is going to be pissed."

"Fuck her, she can't do anything to me."

Two days after I've left, get my first call. Gotten used to the phone lying mute, jump when it rings. It's Roger, nervously telling me that he'd be honored if I'd see him at eleven. He's so relieved I'm open, couldn't bear the thought of never seeing me again.

In a daze not unlike a first date as I smoke a cigarette, feet creaking over the floorboards as I wait for the coffee to drip. Pick out a perfect outfit to christen my apartment—Lucite and black stilettos and thigh-highs with seams up the back, leather skirt. Silk ribbon purple corset caresses my waist, leather bustier completes. Pull my hair into a severe bun (curve of neck so understated), just enough makeup and I'm ready.

Roger rings promptly at five to eleven and Averna stands by the elevator waiting. Door opens and he's so eager. Saw him five or six times in The Studio. Another one in his mid-forties, job too boring to remember. Usual bland fetish of spanking and being told how weak he is.

"You look beautiful, Mistress."

"Thank you, Roger. I know."

"Oh yes, ma'am, I'm sure you do. I have a house-warming, or should I say, dungeon-warming present for you." Holds out a shoebox, opens it to reveal seven-inch Betty Page/Joan Crawford shoes in black soft leather; not cheap.

"Thank you, Roger. You're such a good slave." Blushes to the top of his comb-over. Amazing that they're embarrassed over something like hair, but can brazenly ask for a cock up the ass.

"Thank you, ma'am."

"Why don't we get started? Place the tribute on the shelf." Puts the money where I command, quickly undresses, then on his knees, the consummate good boy. Wonder if he's a sub with his wife or does he yell at her for not impressing his business partners (I'm his redemption)? Does he marvel at how well she's kept her figure, or does he point out the cellulite on her ass? Even if he doesn't, bet he thinks about it when he sees the twenty-year-olds in the secretarial pool. Scum is scum.

Eye on him the whole time as I reach for the paddle. He's going to be here for an hour; won't be any fun if he's useless too soon.

With his ass in the air, make him count off each time I strike. Hold out until fifteen before I stop, stand up. "I think you're ready for the bamboo cane."

"Mistress?"

"Yes?"

"I've never had that used on me."

"Well, there's a first time for everything, isn't there?"

"Yes, ma'am. If you say so, ma'am." Like all the others, easy to put in his place.

Take the cane off its hook, slight weight betraying the pain it can inflict. Stand to his side so if he looks down and back he can just see the tops of my feet. Then the satisfying sound of the bamboo against the air. "You hear that, boy?"

"Yes, ma'am." Very small voice.

"Good," extending the vowels. Shift my knees so they're slightly bent, resting my weight on my heels as I raise my arm (but not high, not yet); thwap. Jerks forward and only color interrupting his pasty white body is a scarlet stripe, diagonal across his ass. Yes, yes—this is what excites me.

"What do you say, slave?"

"Thank you, Mistress," sputters through the sting radiating from the narrow ribbon.

Stop long enough for the pain to begin to recede before hitting him twice more on his thighs, until his knees give way. Pushed to the point where he'll either explode or pass out. Or cry. "I can't take it anymore, Mistress. Please, I need a break."

Lower my arm, pat his head. "I suppose, since you've been so good. As a reward I'll let you worship my feet before I use the cat-o'-nine."

"Oh wonderful, Mistress. You're my dream come true," as he crawls over. Watch him lick the platform, think about how I have to invest in a throne or maybe a bench. Something in black leather. Tentative tip of tongue glides along the top. Boldened, starts kissing all over, caressing the heel with one hand.

Let him almost finish the second shoe before I step back. "That's enough."(Always leave them wanting.) Nods, accepting his so difficult lot in life. Soon he'll be dressed and gone, and will shuck it all off like water on a raincoat.

Pick up the cat-o'-nine.

Will act as if he's never heard of a dungeon, never heard of *Vault*, which he buys every Monday at the newsstand in a neighborhood where he's sure he won't be recognized, slipping the latest issue between two accordion files in his briefcase as he collects his change.

Hit him. Hard.

During his lunch hour, takes the magazine into an impersonal bathroom stall, circling the ads of girls he wants to call, writing (in code, so the wife won't find out) their names and numbers on pieces of paper he slips into his wallet, before jerking off.

My arm loses precision as it picks up speed.

Where's my release? At the end of it, he's still the boss. That's the way they've set it up. Hit him harder as I think about this, no more grunts, just deep exhales as the familiar rhythm of leather against skin lulls me and I wonder if housewives locked in suburbia fantasize about doing this. Would I have dreamed about this if I'd stayed in Priory?

Cat hits the middle of his back over and over again.

Would I have married Lex or Andy and gone over to Marcus and Justine's for Sunday dinner (because if I was there that night, Marcus would have never died)? Before I can dissolve the image of Marcus, realize I was so in love with him that I never saw how he used me (Karen would've been the only one who never did). That night on the playground was nothing but a way to get even. Spent so many years mourning, worshipping him, and I never stopped to think that I meant nothing to him. Even Marcus. Even fucking Marcus.

He slumps forward, then stops moving. Oh Christ, fuck. Lean down to check his pulse but there is none.

Fuckfuckfuck. My first time wasn't supposed to be like this. I wanted to choose.

Calm, calm. What's done is done as I stare at the body already looking waxy. Can't take it back, have to deal with the now. Call 911 and explain? Accidents happen all the time. But then there will be cops. What if they don't believe me, charge me with murder? Need to think.

Kick off my shoes (relief), head into the bedroom, grab a smoke from the pack off the dresser. Parallel thoughts running through my head, need to be logical. Little rationality in wave after wave of rapture. (I am God.)

Open the freezer and take a swig of Dev's vodka. Don't need it, but seems the thing to do. Think, think, lower my shoulders, take full breaths. Chuckle at the brilliance, louder, tears streaming down my face and onto the body as I stand over it.

Think.

No one tells anyone that they're going to visit a dominatrix. His secretary may have marked off the time in his datebook, but not where he was going. What would he say to the boys in the office, boardroom, gym? "Hey, do you like getting beaten and fucked up the ass, too?" For sure he didn't tell his wife. Bet he didn't tell anyone at all.

Another swig warms me. This is the Meatpacking District–John Does show up here all the time. Overhanging steel awnings running along the truck bays recessed into shadows, perfect for a switchblade in the back for the unfortunate soul who dares wander too far west searching for cheap thrills. When they do find his body, what will they think? Something went wrong while he was trying to score drugs, or while picking up one of the transvestites.

No more sessions today as I change clothes. Hand on the box that holds the weed, but have to be on top of this, all there. Chain-smoke instead as I call all my appointments, telling them that there's a flood in the apartment, have to reschedule, of course at a reduced fee to compensate for the inconvenience. Watching the body as I speak with my polite voice, half-hoping he'll suddenly get up.

Have to get it out of here. Open the closet, cabinets, looking for something; my blanket is too thin, overnight bag too small. Frustrated, light another cigarette and stare at the body on the rug. The rug! Phonebook, find Abe's Discount Rugs in lower Chelsea, not too far of a walk.

Head out, ignoring the homeless guy in front of the building saying, "Hey baby, nice ass," instead of using the heel of my palm to splinter the bridge of his nose. Walk north, then east, realize that I have no way of getting the rug back home, much less getting him out in it.

Remember Odd Lot is on Fourteenth. Loop down, get the biggest wire shopping cart they have, plus duct tape. Wheel it all up to Chelsea, and if Abe thinks it's strange that I'm not picky about the color, he doesn't say anything. Shove the rug into the cart.

Minutes later back in the apartment and it's just me and him; sole sound of crossing the wooden floor as I circle and plan. I'm on my own—you live alone and you die alone and you are the only person you can trust in the end.

Lay out the rug, try to drag the body. Lots of grunting and kicking to get it to the edge. Finally able to roll it up, wrap it with tape.

Putting it into the cart is even harder. Ignore the burn in my muscles (for once, wish that I worked out), lifting the top part to the edge of the cart, but it keeps tipping over from the uneven weight. Giving into gravity, lay the cart on its side and try to push the body in, but I can't even lift it.

Worried I'll have to cut it up, last idea before I buy a butcher's cleaver is to unroll a long strip and lay it on the floor. Sit the body up, then lean on it until it folds in half. Knee on his back as I wrap with tape until he stays in place. Using all my weight, able to push him into the cart. Foot on the bottom and with the wires digging into my hands, bruising them, I get it upright, then wheel it to the elevator. Take it downstairs, hollow metal echoing all the way up the shaft.

Outside it's dark as I cross the West Side Highway, under the long abandoned "El," few cars (stripped) marking my path. Walk over the threatening-to-crumble dock, new plastic wheels thump-thumping over the slats, wind pushing most of the water's odor toward Jersey.

Don't pause for quiet reflection before tipping the cart into the green-black Hudson. As I step back onto the concrete, no cops come out of the shadows to slap cuffs on me; no helicopter spotlight shines down. Consider going out for a celebratory drink (first step to avenging Karen), then decide against it.

Once back inside, get undressed, nakedness throwing shadows across the apartment. Take the cat-o'-nine, douse it with rubbing alcohol and lay back on the futon, spreading my legs apart, knees touching my chest. Grab my breasts, squeezing both nipples just hard enough. Rub the handle across my chest, leather tails treading across my skin. Trace it along my thighs, evoking the last hit that got him; looped and each time, wetter. Slowly let the handle slide in, rubbing and pressing against the outer and then inner lips.

Been too long since I've had sex; pressure on my walls, stretches to get the tip in. Spread my legs out even more, flip my hand on the handle—so slowly in and out—while my other hand teases my clit. Slick quickly, vision from reliving how the session should have gone. Strapping on, I would have kneeled behind him, spread his ass cheeks open roughly and guided my head in without any lube. As soon as I put both hands on my hips, Roger's skin turns younger and softer, into Grok, before the image fully forms into my ideal everyman—long hair (black), soft features, strong but lean muscles.

Harder as I move the handle in and out of me. Push him down to the floor, knees on either side of him. "Yeah, fuck yeah." Take control of him, on him, all of him. Before it can go any further, I come hard, making a mess all over the bed. Pass out with the whip in my hand.

Wake up the next day feeling different, whole. Easy to push Roger out of my head so that no one can read it in my eyes; think about anything else (the new Stoli ad I saw on the side of the crosstown bus; if it'll rain tomorrow). See the day's four clients armed with the simple knowledge that I control their breathing, their very existence (no Evelyn to save them). Every moment they live is because I let it happen.

Antsy by the time the last one leaves. Decide to go to Coney, even though there's more than a good chance I'll run into Dev, certainly people we both know. Let everyone see me, what do I have to be ashamed of? Draw the eyeliner a little harder on my lids and head out.

Maybe I'm imagining it, but people seem to stare then veer away from me as I head east. Like they know I'm someone they shouldn't look at for too long. Good. Fuck 'em.

Lights of St. Mark's sparkle, busy in the hazy twilight, last remaining open stalls with rows of sunglasses and medallions gleaming. Weave through the pretty background and take a deep breath, open the door. Another mixed DJ night, not too crowded. A few people dancing to the Clash, good crowd by the bar. Don't feel like dancing yet, go downstairs, order a rum and coke and stand by the benches.

Still on my high, aware of everything from everyone—glistening sweat, cigarette smoke spilling out of their mouths, bodies moving toward me and then away. Feel like I can see their heartbeats, artery in the temple of the purple-haired beauty by the pole in the back.

Bump into Pamela, Dev's ex-bandmember's ex-girlfriend, coming out of the bathroom and we chat about a new group I should really check out. Can't remember their name, but she'll remind herself to tell me when I see her again, and am I going to the Furious George gig this weekend at the Continental? When I'm looking around, lock eyes with Aysh, who's got some generic hottie, not Leaf, hanging off him. He drags her over before I can break away, cuts between Pamela and me.

"You know, Dev's looking for you."

"I'm sure," deliberately exhaling in his face.

"You gonna, like, call him or something? Or are you just going to leave it like that? He's really a fucking mess."

"Aysh, have I ever gotten involved with you or the mother of your baby?" He sneers, bimbo undisturbed. "It's none of your fucking business," I say.

"You need to call him."

"What's done is done. Now, unless you have something else to say to me, which I don't think you do, leave me alone." Don't realize my arm is cocked until I finish speaking.

Shakes his head, pulling the girl behind him by the hand.

"Wow, what was that about?" Pamela asks, "What happened between you and Dev?"

"Nothing. Listen, I'd better go. I'll call you, OK?"

Not too long (or not long enough) before the high of killing has worn off and I'm bored again, then resentful, worse than before. Try to convince myself that maybe I had to get it all out of my system, that Roger was the fallout.

Buy the *News* and *Post* every day looking for an article about a respected businessman disappearing. But there's nothing, no police poking around the bins, no "Eyewitness News" feature. Another story extinguished in the Big City.

Concern of getting caught fades, start to really think about things again. This time is different because not only do I have the want—also know I can.

New guy calls off of one of my ads. Sounds typically nervous as I tell him yes, we have a full array of toys, and yes, I can certainly fulfill any fetish he may have. Enough money's coming in that I was able to buy a steel and leather fabricated throne off an ad in the back of *Hellfire Magazine*, bars on the bottom and sides to double as restraints.

Jason, Paul, Chris, whatever he calls himself shows up right on time. I like that, doesn't think the world revolves around him. Youngish and cute, wearing black turtleneck and black pants, stylishly messed-up hair. Nice break from the three-piece-suit set.

Looks me up and down, relieved the photo didn't lie. (All the new ones do that.) "You may be the most beautiful mistress I've ever had a session with." Usher him in, heard it too many times to respond. "You mentioned on the phone that you were particular about your...wishes?"

"Yes, Mistress. I'd like—no, I need you to humiliate me. Whip me, beat me. I need to feel pain at your hand. Also...may I ask if you do anything more...exotic?"

"Exotic?" Why do they always think that their fantasies are so special?

"Well, I read this story about play piercings, and it got me terribly excited. All I could imagine was how it would feel to be pierced over and over. Was wondering if you were equipped for that."

"I can accommodate you." Actually picked them up last week because of a request from someone who called off my ad and never showed up. Thinnest needles are slid into the first few layers of skin. Looks a lot worse than it feels but he's right, it is hot to see, all those slivers lined up.

"And then, ma'am, I was hoping we could finish with the worst humiliation of all."

Worst humiliation of all? Guy's language is getting on my nerves. He sees my face and says, "You know, dildo training."

"Ah, the worst humiliation. Today's your lucky day. I specialize in that. Tribute is two hundred, which you can give me now; then get undressed and kneel over there."

"I think I found the perfect mistress," as he counts out the bills.

"Don't say that until you're done."

Know he's next as I put the money in the bedroom. Shouldn't my first real one be beautiful (or the closest I can get) instead of some pudgy businessman? Can't (don't want to) hold back and isn't his life as worthless as the next?

Body electrifies, senses sharpen again like they were after Roger. Tingling as I stop in the kitchen (rustle of him taking off his clothes), take the slimmest knife from a drawer, slide it in the side of my high-heeled boot. Careful not to get cut as I walk back out. Not done getting undressed, balling his socks in his shoes, giving me the chance to hide the knife in the closet. Now that I know it won't be an accident this time, want to record every muscle twitch, every involuntary sigh in my mind. Take out the rope.

"Walk over to the Cross and face out." Without clothes, he's much better looking. Sinewed legs, hint of ribcage under defined lats. Only thing separating him from my fantasies is his face. Can work out forever but the face never changes. Cheekbones just shy of prominent, jaw too strong, enlarged pores dotting the skin.

Tie him easily, blindfold. "It'll make the sensations...more sensational," breathe into his ear as I slip it on.

"You think of everything."

Without warning, I hit him, tails landing against hard muscle; definite sound that doesn't come from flab. The abused skin quickly gets puffy, barest trace of welts.

"You like that, boy. You know why?"

"Why, ma'am?"

"Because you're a sniveling little worm. I love watching how pathetic you are when you want it. And I know you want it, bitch. My bitch."

"Yes, ma'am."

"I know. Look, look at that shriveled cock. Do you fuck your girlfriend with that excuse for a cock?"

Wasn't expecting that one. "Yes, Mistress."

"You should be ashamed of yourself. You need to go home and beg her forgiveness for making her condescend to fuck that cock. If I had a cock that size, I wouldn't even take it out at the urinal. I'd sit down to pee. You're just a worthless little scumbag. That's why you had to come here and beg for your punishment." Swing the tails, harder on his legs, arm, then against his balls, cock reddening so hard it bounces. "See, I know what you need."

Groan. "Oh, oh, ma'am, you do."

"Know what I'd like to see?"

"No..."

"I'd like to see you with needles all over that pretty body of yours. I want to see you in pain."

"Yes, Mistress."

Make a lot of noise taking the box out of the wardrobe. "And later, I will give you the final proof of how disgusting you are." Licks his lips, thinking I'm talking about the dildo.

Remove one of the slivers from the tissue paper wrapping; slide the breath of metal easily into the first layer right above his hips, silver lines raising the smallest dot where I've pierced the skin. He's moaning now and totally erect. Getting hot as his breath catches, knowing how bad he wants it. Almost as bad as I do. Soon, they're all lined perfectly to just under his armpits. It's so striking I want to cry.

Fingernail from the bottom of his neck down to just above his pubic line. "Is that enough, or do you want more, boy?" Think for a moment that maybe I shouldn't kill him, that this is one I want to keep coming back. Biting my lip not to flick my tongue over his nipple and make him sigh, my creation. But, I know he'll never be as beautiful as he is now.

"More, please." Then gasps as I puncture the sensitive skin on the inside of his thighs, able to feel the damp between my legs, nipples hard. Too soon, I've used all hundred and fifty needles.

"You look so good like that. Good enough to fuck."

"Oh, Mistress."

"But not yet, boy." Slide the needles out, one by one. Spots of blood show as he winces, shuddering, straining; face flushes as his brain overloads. Taking all of my energy not to slide his strong cock (so hard it looks as if it's about to pop off) into my pussy, wetter than it's been since my last fantasy.

Strap myself in and grab the lube, wave my hand in front of his face to make sure he can't see before I pull the knife out from my boot. So much power radiating that it's bouncing off the walls. Step in close.

"You ready to be my bitch?"

"What about...?"

"What about your shriveled cock? No, I won't let you please yourself. You forgot little boy, you're on my time. No, no, I'm just going to fuck you." Belly to belly, length of my cock nestles just inside the crack, sliding until it reaches the small opening of his asshole, then press. Too hot, fucking him from the front, spreading his cheeks. Close enough to see the creases on his lips, neck and chest arching, whimpers as if he were a virgin.

"See, boy," using my thigh muscles. Easing in, he slowly opens up. "Oooh. You like that? You like that, slut?" We're merging, couldn't be closer, as I'm holding back, holding back, until I can't anymore. Take off his blindfold and his eyes are rolling into the back of his head, sweat dripping off the ends of his hair as he bites his lips involuntarily.

"Oh yeah. Oh, oh," he groans as I look into his eyes. Lift my leg (so gone he doesn't notice anything), take the knife from behind my back. Slide my cock out stroking his neck, wet lips on his sweaty, hairless chest as I slide just enough of the tip of my knife into his loose asshole as he freezes.

"Shush," as he tightens. "Don't make me cut you." Everything is still except for the slight movement of my wrists pushing through soft tissue. Oh yeah, I fuck 'em good.

As I raise the knife again, first stream of blood runs over the tops of my fingers and then down my palms, as he shouts. Dark red, warm, drip, drip onto the floor (what cleans that off of hardwood?). Bring my lips to his as I turn the knife. All paths converging.

Fucking him with the blade, in and out, in and out. Soon, red's staining my boots, the floor, the Cross. I've cut something open, because the blade goes in and out more easily. Kiss the side of his neck, beaded with sweat.

"Humiliated enough?"

Tongue along his eyelids, across his cheeks, over his lips; feel his shallow breath on mine, his dying energy sliding down my throat until I slide the knife in as far as I can without losing it inside him and he dies.

Don't want to break the moment. He looks so beautiful like that, hanging there, blood still dribbling out of his lifeless body just like in my dreams. Hot all over again and I want to strip in front of him and lie down, but I have another appointment in an hour and a half.

Focus, no time to linger. Get two of the heavy black garbage bags left over from the move, cut them under the body and untie his wrists but not his ankles so I can lower him down in a controlled manner. He flops around anyway, spraying more blood, but once he's on the heavy plastic, not too hard dragging him into my bedroom to be dealt with later on. Jump into the shower to rinse off, but the bathroom has blood in it now and I'll have to shower again after I'm done cleaning.

Naked and pinning my hair up, takes nearly half a roll of paper towels to mop up the blood on the floor, trail leading to the bedroom. Of course it won't easily come up, smearing all over. Still traces in the bathroom's white grout even after scrubbing with ammonia. Sprint to the corner store on Tenth and pick up bleach. Get on my knees and go over the entire place again, just to make sure.

Remaining three clients, if they notice anything wrong, don't say or show it. Keep following their line of vision, see if they notice a smudge, a blot I've missed. After the last one leaves, smoke a cigarette, have a bourbon and soda before getting to work. Take the butcher knife (Dev's) into the bedroom, body now very gray, though the flesh is still pliable enough to poke at. Need to be exact (don't want to spray again) and use as much force as I can with little movement cutting; have to use the knife sharpener more than once.

Takes awhile to chop it into pieces. Skin's tough. Except for the head, which I won't try. Stuff the pieces into the extra garbage bags I got when I bought the bleach. Cut tiny slits in the bags, not so big a finger joint could come out, but enough to let it sink.

After showering again, clean again, ammonia cutting through the smell. Don't want to look at the bags now. Even in death they take up space, impose on me. Cursing for not thinking ahead about how to get rid of him; this is the shit that will get me caught.

Drag the bags one by one down to the river. It's been raining, so no one is out except for a shadow of a figure under one of the truck bays, flame from his disposable lighter stopping and starting, glow of crystal rocks in a glass pipe. If he notices anything, probably thinks I'm one of his hallucinations.

In the morning, make coffee, turn on my phone. Two appointments —a new one and Terry, who tips well. Message from Lila, wanting to know if I want to hang out with her and Cleo tonight, mentions that Susan might be there. Haven't been out since running into Aysh.

Call her back and she says hello as if she thought she wasn't going to hear from me. Chat for a few, find out Evelyn's pretty pissed since she saw my ad, though I'm not the first one of her "superstars" to leave. Tells me that they're going to the Pyramid tonight, mentions again that Susan's asked about me, tell her I'll see her later.

Dress in boots, stretch jeans, buckle leather bra and beat-up MC, and head to the club a little after midnight, streets empty except for a hooker or two, drunken Chelsea boys wandering too far south. Stroll east, enjoying a cigarette in the cool air before hopping into a taxi the rest of the way to Avenue A.

Lets me off in front of the club. A few people I don't know are flirting, exchanging phone numbers under the neon glare of the sushi restaurant next door. I recognize the security guard, Patrick.

Gives me a big hug, asks me where I've been; shrug. "Busy, you know." Stamps my hand to drink and opens the door for me; give the new girl at the till my five bucks, go inside.

As faces focus in the dim glow of Christmas lights strung on the walls, realize that hanging out here could be a mistake; more than one person Dev and I know are around. Run my fingers through my hair. You were expecting this. Straighten my back. They can't do anything to you—you're above them.

At the packed bar order a beer because they water down their drinks, and as I'm sliding the tip across feel a tap on my shoulder. Turn around with the glass clenched, ready (wanting) to hit (satisfaction of the glass breaking against cheekbone, star pattern of blood and loose scraps of skin dripping onto the sticky floor). It's Susan grinning at me.

"Hey you. Thought you were gonna call."

"Sorry about that. Been busy lately. Moved out, went into business on my own."

She flips her hair, takes a baby step toward me. "Lila told me. How's that going?"

"It's going."

"Well, come on. I don't want to keep you all to myself until later." Follow her to the piece of wall between the stairs leading down and the men's bathroom where Lila, Cleo and two other girls that I have seen here before are hanging out.

"You made it," Lila says, smiling. "Do you know Therese and Cora? Therese works over at Mistress Judith's and Cora just got hired with us." Wave hi to both of them while Susan stands behind me, tracing imaginary lines on my hips, arms and back with her fingertips while we listen to Therese bitch about how much The Bank's gone downhill.

Quickly drink the beers that Susan buys, trying to avoid eye contact with several people who know Dev and I. Finishing my third beer when Susan says in my ear (red-glossed lips tickling the peach fuzz on my lobes), "I love this song. Wanna go dance?" Put the empty bottle on the lip jutting out of the wall, follow her to the dance floor where they're playing the Depeche Mode cover of "Route 66."

Pressed against each other and by the time the song ends and Billy Idol begins, we're kissing softly (so different than a guy—not as insisting, more comfortable), tongue darting over skin leaving a glossy trail. Toss my head while one hand travels up her back, other just above her ass, which feels as good as it looks. Half-crouch, kiss her sweaty stomach, lick the salty skin, hand on her ribs holding me to her as I move up, run my lips along the bottom of her bra.

"Let's go to the couches downstairs," and we move, my hands on her waist, past Lila and the others without a word (though Cleo lifts an eyebrow and smiles) into the low-ceilinged room with a tiny bar in the corner, even tinier dance floor, couches dotting the walls.

Nobody's DJing down here. Instead there's a pre-mixed CD playing older punk (Iggy Pop, The Cult, Ramones), which I like more anyway. Fall onto the battered, overstuffed loveseat; only others are the bored bartender and two girls dancing on opposite sides of the black-and-white linoleum.

Susan sits while I straddle, cupping a breast with one hand, other in her hair, but there's none of the rush of before (clinical). Arms wrap my hips, wanting me. My rationale betrays my skin and fingers moving against soft flesh through the cotton, reaching for the hard nipple, which I tease with two fingers while pushing away the idea of biting it off, then cutting her skin so gently she doesn't realize until she's flayed, groaning and kissing me in the same desperate way as I peel her like a grape, eating her pussy, slick with her own blood.

Kissing deeper, trying to envelop though I know no matter how talented her fingers are, no matter how much I'd like to see her face in between my legs while coming all over her lips, it's pointless.

Other hand moves down the slim body, trace down her side to her low-slung black pants, gently pressing the soft skin under her belly button. She suddenly breaks away from the kiss. "I want you to take me home tonight." Keep making out, hand sliding between her pants teasing the crack when someone clears their throat over "Detention Home." Ignore it. Only when I hear the familiar "Cassie" do I sit up.

Dev's standing with a look telling me he's been there for awhile.

"Is this what you left me for? This bitch?"

"No, I left you for you. Because you were so fucking pathetic, you couldn't even get me off anymore." Not entirely a lie.

"Is that why you cleared out the apartment? Left me with your hospital bill?"

Stick my chin out. "No, I did that because you owe me."

"Owe you for what?"

"Putting up with your bullshit." Always his selfish agenda, just took awhile to see. Like my father, wanted me to live my life according to his plan. But he was worse, much worse than all of them. He gave me hope, made me open myself.

"Oh, sure. My bullshit. What planet are you from?" Shakes his head, never taking his eyes off of me. "Aysh was right, it's better this way. You're not human anymore, Cass."

No, I'm beyond human.

Susan steps forward. "Why don't you leave her alone? Fuck off."

"Stay out of this."

"What the fuck are you going to do, pretty boy?"

"I told you to stay out of this. Nice choice of company, Cass."

"At least it doesn't sicken her to look at me." She grabs my hand. "Let's go, Cassie. I wouldn't want to waste a night in jail over this loser." Pulls me outside without stopping to say good-bye to anyone. So cute that she's being protective. Who's going to protect her from me?

Into near-empty streets, not slowing our pace until we're on First.

"That your ex?" she asks, pulling out a Marlboro Light.

"Yeah, I guess he's still upset."

"Did you really clean out his apartment?"

"There's a lot of shit...sometimes men deserve it."

"Forget about him," as she leads me toward her building, up the stairs to her apartment. When we get inside, leans me against the front door, kissing, saliva running down our chins, bruising our lips before the familiar feeling gurgles and I want to push her on the floor, slam her head until she passes out and I can have my way...no, not yet, not here. Who knows if the neighbors will be listening through the paper-thin walls, if Lila and Cleo noticed we left together?

Break away as she stares at me. "I gotta go."

"Why?"

"I'm not feeling well. Room's spinning."

"I can get you a glass of water."

"No, I'd better go home." Step out the door, promise to call, her standing perplexed by the sink. Not fucking is a small price to pay for my greater good.

Walk the length home, clear my head, knowing I can't see her, any of them, again.

Walking to the bagel place every morning and buying the papers becomes routine. Nothing in months aside from a small article near the sports section of the *Times* about Thomas Lehland, fifty-eight, of the Upper East Side; his wife a well-known socialite. Found in a dumpster near Bellevue, strangled. Doesn't mention the castration, face slashing and disembowelment. No leads in the case.

No articles about the others. Two are in the bottom of the Hudson where they'll never be found, soft tissue probably already eaten by chemicals and whatever's evolved to survive down there. Another wound up in a pile of snow, plowed so it created a wall blocking the narrow sidewalk on Little West Twelfth. Last one dumped in an unused playground on Seventeenth, after being carefully delimbed and put into a cheap suitcase. Slowly getting even.

Spend a lot of time alone in the loft. No one's going to understand me, don't want to relate to others. And I can't trust myself outside. Go to the bodega to get a pack of smokes and picture the old man behind the counter with his throat slit, bleeding all over the nickel candies. At the nameless bar on Twenty-Second, wonder if I can't pop the bartender's eyes open with a beer bottle. Clients are even harder to resist; it's like handing an ex-junkie a syringe.

Masturbate all the time to take the edge off, but it doesn't do much. Can't lash out, know I have to pace myself though my slipping disdain for humanity makes it difficult. The lion does not lie with the lamb.

Cleaning the St. Andrew's Cross I think of Roger, my first, and my other first, another first I can't tell anyone about. Whenever I've been asked, I've always shrugged it off with a "You know, normal."

Jon Wolverly, Spike's cousin from Canton. Skateboard kid, skinnier than me with long brown hair and these huge blue eyes that looked perpetually surprised. We got ice cream and exchanged syrupy marijuana kisses in the woods behind the train tracks. Showed me how to ollie and gave me flowers picked from Mrs. Staveall's yard.

Three or four days before his parents would be taking him back to what seemed at the time a big city, we took a walk to the complex of low concrete buildings that made up the foundry. Kicked the small pebbles as the sun beat through my black T-shirt and we found the person-width alley between two of the structures. Sat down with our knees pressed into our chests, concrete scraping our skin, shared the fifth of vodka stolen from his uncle's liquor cabinet.

When it was gone, I stood and stumbled against the wall, drunker from the late August sun. "I have to go home."

"Wait, I have to tell you something." He touched my wrist, then leaned in to me. Our lips were swollen from making out all weekend every time an adult was out of sight. Head swimmy, sweaty hands over clammy skin as we pulled each other's shorts down. Propping himself up with one elbow as I lay on the hot concrete, blocking out the sun. Hand under my shirt over my bra as I reached down, fumbled over his boxers with his hardening as I tried to keep the sky from spinning.

Don't remember if he asked me or if I silently conceded. But it seemed very (too) quick, and before I could change my mind he was steadying himself, pressing as hard as he could and I was readying for the pain that never came; slid in easily. Looked at me wide-eyed and then narrowed as he pulled out, turned his back as he started getting dressed.

"What's going on?"

"You told me you were a virgin."

"I am a virgin."

"Where's your cherry, then? You opened your legs like someone who's done it before."

"I swear I've never done it." Sudden sobriety, crying now. "I don't know why I don't have one." But I did know (Mrs. Manchester's came rushing back as hard as I'd pushed it away) and he saw it.

"You slut," before tearing off.

Blindly found my way home, where I ignored my parents

banging on the door, demanding we have Sunday dinner like a normal family. Hid in my room the last two weeks of summer, positive that everyone in town was having a laugh at my expense, that if I stepped into the street I'd be pointed at, called a whore. Made my mother tell Marcus and Justine that I had the stomach flu when they came to pick me up for Jaime's Last Weekend of Summer party.

Was finally forced out the door for the first day of school. Lex saw me by the side entrance sneaking a cigarette during the bell before study hall and I couldn't avoid it anymore. If they knew, they didn't embarrass me with it. But I always felt branded, another wall built with secrets, no way to tell anyone the truth. Try to push these things out of my mind, erase the memories.

He's my last session of the day. A regular of Victoria's at The Studio, he'd always meant to take a session with me, and when he saw I'd gone independent had to call. (Wonder why they even bother to explain themselves.) Very casual, mid-forties, thinks he's better-looking than he actually is. Suspenders, wire-rimmed glasses, drinks white wine at the charity balls I imagine his wife drags him to. Tells me we met during a meet and greet, surprised I don't instantly recognize him. Makes sure I see his diamond cuff links. Bondage, light (he stresses) humiliation, punishment.

Though his attitude would usually grate, am in an especially good mood. Got the phone call before he showed up that not only did I get the cover of *Rapture*, I'm also going to be a "featured mistress" in *Fetish International*. Even with my own particular fetish, there's no shortage of dupes and I now have a waiting list, thinking of raising my hourly rate.

"How long will you be staying?"

"It really depends on how...much of you I get to see. I'll start with a half hour and if you're any good, I'll take another half." No one's spoken to me like that in so long, almost ask him to repeat himself. Ready to grab him by his scruff and toss him on his ass, but stop. So he can think of me as a cunt, go someplace else? I don't think so. This one will be fun. "I understand. You're a very busy man."

Undressed, he stares at my thighs until the snap of me pulling on latex gloves gets his attention.

"What's that for?"

"You'll find out." For some variety, put him on his knees, wrists and ankles tied behind. As I finish my knots, he asks, "Are you sure you've been in this business long? I prefer an experienced mistress."

"Oh yes, I'm sure."

When he's secure, mask shatters. No more pretense of niceties, dumb fuck looking right at me and doesn't realize. So absorbed, right in his face and he still thinks he's untouchable. Raise my heel and kick him in the shoulder, tipping him over. Finally looks at me, shocked (or because I've crossed his ego?) but still going along with it.

"You think you're so much better, huh? Paying to bottom from the top. You think you're the first to try it? Well, you picked the wrong mistress to fuck with." Then that he realizes this won't be the regular session and starts to yell, which makes me laugh.

"No one can hear you, asshole." Kick him harder, in the mouth this time and he bleeds from the corner of his lips, crimson trail running down his neck.

"You fucking bitch," as he spits out pieces of teeth.

"What, do you think you can just order me around? Like you do your secretary? Your wife?" Kick him in the ribs at the end of each sentence.

"You won't get away with this." Winces as he breathes.

"You tell anyone you were coming here, asshole? Think they'll search high and low for you?" Reality of it collapses on him. Face contorts in panic, eyes wild as he tries to inch, tied up, toward the elevator. An hour ago he was invincible. How the mighty have fallen.

Watch and laugh as I take five steps and I'm in front of him.

Bash his head on the floor, knocking him on his back like a bloody cockroach. No other kind of lesson will teach him. Red seeps in even more as I think about how he's probably done it his whole life (so the type to chase his secretary around her desk). Sent to prep school, fast track to whatever Ivy League his father and grandfather went to. Another leech, doesn't deserve to take more from this world than he already has.

Hit and kick over and over, ribs, face, legs until he stops moving. Look down, out of breath. He's semiconscious, moaning, breath shallow from the cracked ribs. Perfect.

I've gotten stronger since Roger; hardly strain dragging him to the middle of the room. High off the rage, looking down at the broken body that I've created; deep swollen bruises an aphrodisiac. Ultimate putty in my hands. Spread out like a blank canvas, an unwilling sacrifice. Waiting for him to come around so he can feel all of it.

Grab the knife after changing quickly; no point in getting my work clothes dirty. Must have hit him good because I am able to have a screwdriver and cigarette while waiting for him to move.

Finally, head jerks and he winces. Pad back to him in my bare feet and straddle him, resting on my elbows. Eyes are almost swollen shut, black and deep purple; gorgeous blood from cuts on his scalp (bright red oozing). "Cunt," he tries to say, comes out as "cunnk."

"Yes, yes I am," as I make sure he can see the blade through his eye slits; quick cut along what was once highish cheekbones but is now pulp.

"Please, I'll do anything. You can have my money. I have money."

"I don't want your blood money. I want you." Punch him hard in the face and he coughs on the liquid running down his throat. Switch hands and slash his other cheek as my breath melts on his lips and he yelps, jerks.

On my knees, eyes riveted; so close, as if we were lovers. Blubbers like a baby, as if him crying will make me realize, put the knife down and untie him. Probably crocodile tears anyway. No matter if it never really fills the hole in my stomach, if the weight that I couldn't protect her never leaves my shoulders.

Take out garbage bags from the kitchen cabinet. Cut, slide them around him, not caring that he can see, let him know that these are his dying moments. Let him regret, and wonder what could have been, what he'll never do. Catch the blood before it stains the floor. Took me so long last time to get the mess up.

Shove his face back with the heel of my hand and slice the back of his head, blade so fine it takes a moment for the wound to open on his scalp; elegant marks inflicted like brushstrokes. Put down the knife and light a smoke, go at my own speed. No threat now, groaning, coughing on his own blood. Garbled pleading as I ash on him, then "Fuck you" when he realizes begging won't help.

Extinguish the butt out on his shoulder. Cries and tries to wiggle away, rocking back and forth. More shallow cuts on his chest, watching the layers of skin, fat, muscle, the way it waves fluidly as he strains. Silence now, like he's going to take it like a man. Can read his thoughts: "My father was a soldier and so was my grandfather. I can take you, just untie me. And while you may kill me, bitch, you can't take my pride." Shake my head. They lie even to themselves.

Rest my crotch against his thigh, lean my whole body against him. "Ooh, baby. Did anyone ever tell you look better bleeding?" Eyes are filming over; even more turned on knowing that I'll be the last image he ever sees, that I won his body and soul as money never could. It was only a few minutes ago he wanted to force his will, his decisions on me. Motherfucker. Slam the knife into his bicep, almost piercing the whole way. Yelps, didn't know he had that much left in him. Guess he wasn't as much of a man as he thought he was.

Push him over so he's lying on his back, hands behind him, raising his ass in the air. Move down, straddle his knees—incision on the underside of his belly where a caesarian would have been, but bigger, like a big bloody smile (Karen smiling at me, I'm doing the right thing). I know what he's done with other women—doesn't strike as the type to take no for an answer. Know what he would do to me, if he could.

Let's see how he likes it. Take the biggest dildo from its place on the shelf and plunge. Incision isn't very wide and he screeches inhumanly as I jam the plastic in and his skin rips and then it's very mushy and soft, feeling behind the shaft almost egg yolky but thicker, as the organs move away. One (stomach? no, too low) won't slide past but I push down anyway until I feel the hardness of the floor beneath us. And it's too much for him, the pussy. Slap him in the face a few times hoping he'll wake, but he's dead. Wanted him to last a little longer, have to be patient next time.

Wrap the garbage bags over his useless weight, and as I'm lighting another cigarette before pushing him into the cart, the phone rings. Annoyed I didn't turn it off, grab it from the counter, finger on the reject button. Caller ID reads "NY Police Department." Freeze and drop it, plastic clattering, cigarette falling beside it. Smell the embers burn the varnish on the floor.

Takes until the cigarette burns itself out before I can retrieve the message:

"Hello Miss...Averna. This is Detective Alvarez at the Nineteenth Precinct. We're investigating a Missing Persons Report and your card was found in the victim's Filofax. Covering all bases here and was hoping you could assist us. Please call us back at 555-0600."

Forty-five minutes pass until I calm myself enough to put the soggy body parts in the black plastic garbage bags (dumping my clothes in, too), and wheel it by the door, to be gotten rid of after the sun goes down.

When I'm done scouring, practice speaking out loud until I think I sound normal. Deep breath dialing the numbers, remind myself that cops are no different from anyone else.

"Alvarez."

"Hello, Detective? This is Averna. You called earlier but I was with a client." If he found my card, he knows what I do.

"Oh, thank you for calling me back." Good, thrown off. "Averna, we're looking for a missing person, Harold Walker. We found his Filofax, and your card was in it."

"I don't recognize the name, Detective, but sometimes clients use aliases. How can I help you?"

"We're trying to get background on the vic...excuse me, missing person. We found out he led a double life, and we need to look at that too."

"I'd be happy to help you any way I can."

"Great. Can you come to our precinct tomorrow, say, around eleven?" First thing that crosses is possession is nine-tenths. Worry that if I get in, I won't get out. Need it on my terms and even though tomorrow's my day off, "I'm pretty booked. I'm open for an hour tomorrow at two-thirty."

"Sure, sure, I understand," and gives me the address. Totally different from the cops at St. Vincent's but then this one wants something. If he didn't, he wouldn't even spit on me.

Next afternoon, there at two-thirty on the dot. Outfitted not obviously—hair down and brushed back, V-neck shirt to show just a hint of breast, blue jeans I forgot I had. Made sure the house was spotless before I left, just in case. Don't know for sure that I killed this guy, though it would be a strange coincidence if I hadn't.

Try to think about anything else (laundry, getting takeout out from the new Chinese place, picking up a smaller ballgag), pretend that I'm a Concerned Citizen as I open the door to the station (painted institutional green). Smells of arrogance and despair, lit too bright; uniformed officers and detectives posing as drug dealers dragging in unwilling would-be customers. Faded cartoon anti-drug and 1-800-COPSHOT posters hang, peeling at the edges between reinforced windows.

Detective Alvarez is chubby, bad suit. All hard but when he comes home he's a teddy bear, loves his wife and kids. His partner's big also, bland and blond with a handlebar mustache, looks like he played football in junior college. Sits at the adjoining green Formica and metal desk making phone calls, pretending not to listen to us. Detective Alverez motions for me to sit down and I do primly.

"Thank you for taking time out of your schedule. Averna? Is that your name?"

"Stage name. My real name is Cassie Chambers."

Scribbles it on a mini-notepad. "Like I said on the phone, we're investigating the disappearance of Harold Walker. Was he a client of yours?"

"I don't recognize the name."

Takes a picture from a recycled manila folder. "Does he look familiar?"

"Oh, sure. That's...Justin. Or, that's what he told me."

"So he was a client of yours? How did you meet?"

"Yes, he was a regular. Called off one of my ads."

"How often did he come in?"

"Every few weeks. One of those who made the rounds."

"Can you tell me what he liked?"

"Spanking, humiliation."

Jots it down. "And when was the last time you saw him?"

Bite a corner of nail and pretend to think, even though I know it was when I was stuffing his head in a cooler. "I have to look at my date book...it must have been a month or so ago."

"Were you wondering why he hadn't come back?"

Girlie laugh. "It's S&M, Detective. Do you really think I gave him a second thought? I figured he started going someplace else."

"I'm sorry to drag you all the way up here. I don't think that we'll have any more questions, but if we do, we'll call."

"Thank you," smile as if this whole thing is a lark, that the real Cassie is just the girl next door.

"Let me ask you something," as he walks me out. "Do you get a lot of clients? I mean, just curious how many guys are into this stuff."

"Detective, you'd be surprised," as I step onto the sidewalk, jump into a cab and wait until we're around the corner to light a cigarette, ignoring the cabbie's coughing.

Too close. If I didn't know before that it was time to get out, I do now. Only needs one more connectionless connection before I'm a suspect. Need to be smarter. No more, must fight it until I figure out a plan. Ignore the other voice telling me the need's gotten too strong, that it's only a matter of time.

Feel like I'm going out of my mind. Jittery, snapping at the clients at inappropriate times. Craving gets worse until it feels so bad I'm waking up in the middle of the night in a cold sweat. Eating at Odessa's, I want to stab the waitress in the neck with the fork when she forgets my coffee, ripping the flesh on her pale neck, opening her jugular with my bare hands so it sprays all over the gray and white walls.

Drinking a screwdriver comfortably in the corner of the not-packed Henrietta on Hudson (not enough energy to trek all the way to Meow Mix) after a long day. Thought the liquor would dull my hunger, but it isn't; voices screeching in my head are pissing me off even more. I'd leave but I know no place will be better, and drinking at home alone, accompanied only by the images of those whose lives I have taken, just seems sad. Drink faster.

Raise my head to order another and a not-bad redhead (deer caught in headlights look?) is staring me up and down. Consider letting her catch my eye, then walking over with whatever clever line; however, too much effort to play the game tonight (mental image anyway of her naked on my bed, open in every way possible). Besides, still fasting. Doesn't mean I'm not tempted (haven't tasted female flesh since stumbling out of Susan's) and as I finish my glass, can't resist a last look as I leave.

Next door at the 24-hour deli, buy a pack of Dunhills, fighting the urge to scald the guy ahead of me with the pot of stale coffee near the magazine rack for paying for his egg salad sandwich with a credit card.

Outside and there she is, affecting cool, a knowing smirk as she leans against an old Buick smoking a Marlboro Light. Look at her as I open my pack, light up. She steps up to me, inhales. "Take me home." Some just beg for it.

Nod and look around, but no one notices us; all the women too busy checking each other out. Follows me one step behind like a puppy, not asking my name or where we're going, only whispering "you're so hot" in my ear every few blocks, breath tinged with rum.

Into my building, her high-heeled boots clacking against concrete on the way to the elevator, leaning into me with her whole body as we ride up, nibbling on my neck as I stand stoically, then lifting her muscular thigh into my hands as we start to kiss; I forgot how much I miss the contact.

Open the apartment door and fall into the front room, concentrating on taking off and dropping her clothes (she's too drunk to notice the setup, maybe she doesn't care). Not a bad body, just curvy enough, hips a little thick (even hotter), as she stands in the doorway of the kitchen, track lighting shining over her breasts and belly. Still clothed I touch her, hands grazing over skin (too dry to be smooth) as I would livestock. Under semi-calloused fingers, her muscles slightly defined, alive, asking for it. Stand as she tries to undress me, shake my head. "No, no. It's all about you."

Ease her onto the futon, thighs between thighs and she's rubbing herself like a bitch in heat. I relent, pressing nipples and pussies frenzily as I devour her mouth with mine. Roll on top, grinding against her. So damp I can feel it against my jeans against my lips and now she's pleading for it with her eyes. Earlobes, neck, collarbone, hot skin cool saliva trail, want to flay her with my teeth.

Groaning like a porn star as I move my mouth over the swell of her breast to her nipple, where I suck hard, catch the stiff softness between my teeth and pull. Smothering in soft, baby-powdered flesh wrapping her legs around my hips, pulling my crotch into hers (trying to chafe her lips on the denim but it doesn't deter), move my hands down the side of her body, firm ass. Kiss, lick down her stomach until I get to trimmed pussy; asking for it even more.

Licking, inhaling; hotter and hotter her slickness against my lips—could eat her up; instead of the thin wet of her come, blood all over my face, body (cleansing me). No, no...can't kill again until I can think of my safety. Shake my head, get it out before my body takes action without my mind's permission.

Lick, suck, playing with the edges of her hole with my fingertips as she's grinding until she comes, spilling all over my chin. Looks down glassy-eyed.

"Oh, God. That was so amazing," she growls. "Your turn now. Come on, show me that beautiful body."

"No baby, I need to fuck that." Moans, thinking of her next orgasm. Stupid.

Grab from the closet the vibrating dildo I bought the other day at Babes in Toyland. Bring it in with my harness and K-Y; she's still lying in a daze, legs spread on my pillow. Not taking her eyes off me, a small smile on her face, like she has one up. She'll see.

Lube up and strap on over my jeans, let her take it in before leaning over the futon. Kiss her soft underbelly, spreading her legs further with both hands. Kneel, rest the head against her hole, press gently until just the tip is in. Such a different sensation than a guy's asshole—small resistance, but inviting, begging me to fuck her till it comes out of her mouth.

Her submissiveness invites me to etch my deepest secrets. Pick up her knees, throw her legs over my shoulders and slowly, so slowly she whimpers, "Please."

"Please what?"

"Please fuck me."

Tingling anticipation. Dig my nails into her palms, bucking her hips up to take in as much of me as she can. Pause when I'm about to go all the way in, then press myself inside her.

And though I've never fucked a chick before, feels so natural. Long and smooth at first, picking up speed as I zone faster, pounding, feeling her give and spread her legs straight out, wanting my cock as she's moaning, writhing. Fucking her like the slut she is.

Lean in, caress her arms, sides and she's breathing heavier (rutting), getting close to orgasm. Up, putting both hands on her shoulders as I go slower and harder, closer to that arched neck, but she doesn't notice. Can't get off any other way; whose orgasm is more important?

Squeeze, driving in even more, ripping her in two, so hard and fast that I'm bruising my hips against hers. Squeeze, squeeze and she realizes I'm not playing games, that maybe going home with someone whose name she never got, that no one saw her talking to, may not have been the best idea.

Plants the palms of her hands, tries to get up. But I'm more muscular than she is, and have her pinned in two places. Keep fucking as I squeeze, her thrashing under me, exerting real effort for the first time in a long while, me groaning in orgasm as she grows weaker, clawing at my arms subsiding, life ebbing between my fingers. Can feel it, harder, harder, deeper—baby, show me that still heart!

Lying limp, staring at the ceiling, distinctive hand marks on her neck (could they identify me that way?). Energy spikes down into immediate wave of exhaustion. Know I should take care of her now, but instead lie back and light a cigarette beside my little martyr.

Idea of her still there in the morning gets me moving. Push her into the cart and like so many times already, cut small holes in the bag so that she sinks.

Shitshitshit, as I push the package into the black water (rough tonight, pounding against the rotting wood), walk back. Can't stay here any longer. Only a matter of time before some infinitesimal fiber connects me. Gone are the Boston Strangler, *In Cold Blood* days where a murder could be committed in the next town, next state and it would be months or never before police could make the connection. Not like that anymore. And I'm not so arrogant to think I'm smarter than all cops. No way to know if they found the bodies and just kept it out of the press.

Don't even have a passport. Doesn't it take, like, six weeks to get one? And what if they do finally figure it all out? They could just pull my name up and get me. Fuck that, gotta be fake. Tick through my head who I could ask...Lucas—Lucas would be the person to talk to.

Next afternoon cab it to Broadway and Eighth, walk across Astor to St. Mark's. Lucas is always somewhere along the strip between Third and A. If I wait long enough he'll eventually traipse up.

Today it's two cups of coffee and half a pack of cigarettes before I see him, loping up the block in stoned silence along with a tattoo-faced gutterpunk who looks familiar.

"Yo, Luke." Looks up in the same unhurried way he was walking and waves, waits for me to cross the street. Eyes glazed which is good, means he won't be rushing to cop.

"Hey, girl," leaning down and kissing me on the cheek, so pale I can see the veins in his eyelids. "I haven't seen you in a while. Where you been?"

"You know, around. Working. Listen," voice drops, lean in again. "I wanted to ask you a question."

"Shoot."

"Fake passport."

"What, you in trouble or something?" Don't say anything and, "Yeah, I know a guy. He's uptown. It's gonna cost, though."

"I figured. When can we go?"

"How soon do you need it?"

"Yesterday."

"We can go now, if you want...you'll pay me a finder's fee, right? Like, fifty?" Nod. Everything, everyone has a price.

"All right. Let me call him. You got a quarter?" Dig in my pocket as we go to the pay phone inside BBQ's across the street. He dials. "Hey, it's Lucas, man, Frank's friend. How ya been? Yeah...yeah. I got somebody you may want to meet....Yeah, she's in a hurry. I know the place. We'll be there after she gets her photo. Like an hour?" Hangs up. "We're meeting him at a coffee shop near his place."

Hail a cab outside the "Passport Fotos While-U-Wait." Driver's not happy when Lucas gives him an address in Washington Heights. Don't talk much after we catch up on the local gossip; he's seeing some girl he met at Webster Hall, but she's become a drag. Hot in bed, but told him it was her or coke and didn't she know drugs always come first?

Look out the window at everything, everyone passing. Going about their lives, happily insulated, never thinking outside themselves. I'm doing the world a favor, clearing out the worst who have taken the most, those who kill in their own way.

Driver stops on a corner near a boarded, burned tenement, some kids playing stoopball against the side. We get out, walk into the greasy spoon across the street, outline of where letters making up a sign that once spelled "Bernard's" used to hang. Inside, waitress, Hispanic guy in his late twenties, and a sullen young girl with a withered arm stirring her coffee. Lucas makes a beeline for the guy, who's jabbering away on his cell. Muscle tee though it's a little chilly for it; bad, blurry tattoos, thick black lines.

"How you been, Luke? Haven't seen you in a while."

"Getting by."

"So, what can I do for you?" Smooth.

"My friend here is interested in your specialty."

"How soon?"

"As soon as possible."

"Oh really, *bonita chica*? You need a new identity that soon?" Noncommittal shrug. "Alright, I got you. You took one of those photos?"

Slide it to him.

"Cool. Meet me day after tomorrow here, same time with your boy and two grand." Thought it would be much more.

Start packing as soon as I get home, no reason to wait. Two bags of the clothes I love the most, few books I can't leave behind (mainly the Japanese bondage books and my H.P. Lovecraft collection), some of the more expensive equipment. Everything else can be left for the landlord to deal with. Don't even know where I'm going yet, just going. Maybe leaving will make me forget.

Day after tomorrow. Meet Lucas with bags in hand and he makes a crack that I must be in a hurry, guesses he won't be seeing me again. More concerned about the Franklin, though, which I give him only where we're in the cab.

Back at Bernard's, guy wearing the same muscle tee. Like a movie, I slide the money across in an envelope. I am now Alicia Bayham—birthplace, Chicago.

Waste no time after dropping off an antsy Lucas on Ave. A to cop. "JFK International, please." So that's it, my time here's done, the place of my true birth. Ready to go, any good memories long gone. No pangs knowing I'll never see the inside of The Bank or Mother's again, never walk through Tompkins Square Park at perfect twilight, sound of dogs in the run, sprout of green trees in the gray. It's time.

Thoughts are broken with, "What terminal, miss?"

"Uh, TWA." Drops me off and I drag my bags through the clots of families and tour groups, like any other harried traveler.

Just take the first flight to anywhere that appeals. Scan down the green Departing screen. Rio? Would be pretty but too long to set up shop. Moscow? Hate cold. Barcelona? Maybe.

Last flight listed is London. Could picture myself there, always wanted to check it out. I speak the language, and images of King Arthur and the Sex Pistols dance through my head. Want to see where civilization began, walk along the same water where Julius Caesar once sailed.

Walk to the ticket counter. "One way to London, please."

Agent nods, barely looking at me. "Can I see your passport?"

"Sure," stone-faced at the counter as she looks at it, types the name. Clench my jaw, wait for her to press the big red button behind the counter, guards with guns drawn coming out from every crack to drag me away to the "secret room."

Nothing comes up. Ticket prints and the twit smiles as she hands it to me. "You're in seat 23A. Please be at the gate an hour ahead. Enjoy your flight, Ms. Bayham."

Smile as I walk to the bar to wait, ready to take on the Old World....